FLIGHT TO
FREEDOM

FLIGHT TO FREEDOM

One Family's Escape from Estonia

MARILYN SMITH NEILANS

ISBN 13: 978-1518637773

ISBN 10: 1518637779

Published in the United States of America

By

G J Publishing
515 Cimarron Circle, Ste 323
Loudon TN 37774
www.neilans.com

DEDICATION

Dedicated with love and endless admiration to Jenny Laumets Sikula who has become my good friend as well as the inspiration for this story.

IN APPRECIATION

I owe particular thanks to Jenny's daughter Ku Laumets Adams, who opened my eyes to realities of life that I had not understood or appreciated before; and to Jenny's daughter Tina Sikula Arnett, who opened her home and her heart to me. It has been a rare privilege to know ... and love ... this family.

Thanks also to Rutt Tanev and the rest of the English-speaking staff at the Põltsamaa Visitors' Center and Museum for their many kindnesses and time spent with me on my research trip to Estonia. *Tänan väga.*

And thanks to my husband John, who, as always, was my strength as well as my number one editor and proofreader.   *Marilyn Smith Neilans*

Jenny Laumets and her daughter Küllike

Põltsamaa, Estonia

1944

PROLOGUE

"Mamma! Come! We must go now!" The young woman, having awakened in the very early morning to the steadily increasing rumbling of Russian tanks, felt fear but not panic. She knew now what she must do to protect her young daughter, her mother, and herself; and she was prepared to move heaven and earth to do so.

The evening before, when Jenny had told her mother that one of her co-workers at the Põltsamaa Police station had pulled her aside at the office, whispering urgently: "Hitler has ordered all Germans to evacuate Estonia immediately; the Soviets are returning. All the officers are leaving tonight; they have agreed to take you and your family with them."

The older woman had demurred, saying noncommittally, "Perhaps we should go, but not yet, not yet. When Vaike returns from her girlfriend's house we can all talk about it." Marta had continued, calmly, "It will be okay, Jenny. We will sleep now, and there will be time to pack in the morning."

Now there was no more time for persuasion; she had to act. Jenny grabbed her suitcase, throwing into it anything she could put her hands on, and then did the same for her mother's things. Finally, stooping awkwardly with her suitcase banging her thigh, she lifted Küllike with her other hand, cradling the child's sleepy head against her neck and whispering reassuring words she herself did not believe. "Shh, shh, my baby. Everything will be all right. Sleep again, my darling."

Jenny jerked open the heavy door and was relieved beyond measure to see the familiar big white and blue police truck already turning into their back alley. "Mamma!" she repeated, propping the door open with her foot.

"I'm coming, I'm coming." Marta was grasping her own small bag but rather than moving, she stood quite still, looking about distractedly. "But, Jenny, Vaike is not home yet. Where can she be? We must wait for her."

"Mamma, she will have to find us later. We have to go now." Jenny was already going out the door, passing her bag to the young man who had bounded up the steps to help her. She turned, and with her now-free hand pulled her mother's elbow, almost dragging her down to the alley. Their door swung shut behind them, with an achingly final bang.

PART ONE

Estonia

1920 - 1944

Estonia Wins Her Independence

With the Signing of the Peace Treaty:

"Tartu Rahu"

1920

1

Jenny came hurrying up the back steps and into the kitchen, her dark wavy hair bouncing around her ears. "Mamma, Mamma, look how many berries I brought for you!" She proudly held out a large bucket, filled to the brim with juicy, bright blue berries. "And I sold all the rest before I could even get home. The Kaals and Valdovs and Jürmans each wanted as many as I would let them have … but I kept enough for you to make a yummy dessert for us."

"Those are lovely, Jenny." Marta, who had been mixing red pickled beets into a large bowl of *rosolje*, wiped her hands on her white apron, took the proffered treasures, and set them beside the sink. "But where's your sister?"

"I told her to come on, Mamma. I did." Jenny shook her head. "But she wouldn't. She stayed in the meadow to play with Jaanus and Rein and Julika. You know Vaike never minds me."

Jenny brushed a few twigs and leaves from her skirt, then continued, "I'll go again tomorrow, if the weather stays fine, and this time I'll bring home enough for *Isa* to start a batch of his favorite wine. Won't he be surprised!" When she smiled, her face spread into wide dimples.

****

The lively child was only slightly aware of the fortuitous circumstances that had surrounded her since her birth. Marta and Karl Rissman had welcomed their beloved daughter into the world in 1920, the very year they and their countrymen celebrated the *Tartu Rahu* – the peace treaty that established the independent Republic of Estonia.

Jenny had attended Estonian schools, taught by Estonian teachers, speaking only Estonian. It all seemed very normal.

Her parents, however, knew how precious this statehood was to a country that had been overrun for centuries by competing forces.

2

"Hurry up, now, both of you." Marta was trying to usher the two girls out the door. "We don't want to be late for church this morning!"

Jenny, excited by the Christmas preparations that had been going on in their house for weeks now, finished buttoning her winter coat, grabbed her mittens, and stood impatiently, hopping from one foot to the other as she waited for Vaike to get ready. "I'm ready, Mamma," she announced.

"Vaike! Come along!"

Jenny's younger sister was dawdling in the hall, looking wistfully at the spruce tree set up near their *Isa's* chair. It was already decorated with white candles, and tonight would be the night *Isa* would light them and transform the house into a magic land.

Finally, Jenny marched over to Vaike, tugged on her hand and practically dragged her out the door.

"But I don't want to leave ... I want to be here when *jõuluvana* comes," wailed Vaike."

"Oh, hush. Santa won't come until we get home from church anyway. And you know Mamma won't let us duck services tonight of all times." Jenny called upon her best big sister logic. "So just come on."

But both girls turned eyes filled with longing back toward the tree as Mamma ushered them out the door and into the cold, snowy night.

The beautiful big Lutheran church was built into Põltsamaa's old castle walls. The castle itself dated back to the 13th century, and the section where the services were held had been converted to a church sanctuary in the 1630s. It was magnificent, with a tall steeple dominating the sky above the peaceful village.

Marta seemed almost transfixed by the soaring sounds of the choir's renditions of the familiar hymns, but to Jenny and Vaike they were torture. The pews were hard, straight backed wooden benches, and the cavernous, soaring ceilings and thick stone walls seemed to suck every bit of warmth right out of the cold space.

Plus, the girls knew that when they finally returned home, jõuluvana would come, and the jolly Santa Claus would bring them gifts. Jenny had practiced, over and over, the song she would sing for him, but she still felt a little nervous. *I want my song to be perfect.* She knew that Vaike was supposed to recite a short poem, but she had not heard her practicing it more than once or twice. *Hers won't be perfect, for sure.*

The seemingly interminable services finally came to a merciful end, and the sisters hastily pulled on their woolen coats and rushed outside. Normally they would have played in the snow that powdered the lanes and gardens, but not tonight. Tonight was Christmas Eve!

3

W ell, my Jenny, we have a bit of good news for you. My sister has agreed that you can live with her for the next two years."

Jenny flung her arms around her mother, and then pulled her father into the embrace too. "Dear *Tädi* Frieda! Now it is all really going to happen."

Jenny would be graduating from high school soon, and had long had her heart set on studying at the business school in Tallinn. She had met all the requirements for admission, but the family had been worried about the cost for room and board.

"Now all my planning and studying are going to be rewarded," she continued, breaking into a quick stepping dance around the room.

That evening the lively family seated themselves around their kitchen table, digging into a hearty wiener schnitzel, full of optimism about Jenny's bright future.

Even her younger sister Vaike was in an unusually happy mood, although Jenny knew her cheer had more to do with the fact that the good looking Jaan Aabram had stopped her in the hallway at school. She had confided to Jenny that afternoon that she was sure he had been flirting with her.

****

When Jenny graduated from the Tallinn Business Institute in 1940, she parlayed her skills into finding a secretarial job with the largest insurance company in Estonia, typing and filing and filling out policies with a happy heart, loving life in the big, bustling capitol city – a far cry from little Põltsamaa.

She found love there, too, with the dashing Osvald Laumets.

"Mamma – I've met the most wonderful man! He has asked me out several times. We both enjoy going to the theatre. He's fun, and kind, and so good looking ... "

"Wait, wait, Jenny," Marta interrupted. "What is this 'wonderful' man's name? Where does he work?

How old is he? You know your *Isa* will need to know all these details, too."

"Oh, dear Mamma. Of course. Well ... " She held up the spread fingers of her left hand, and began ticking off details one by one with her right index finger, " ... his name is Osvald Laumets. He is 26 years old and manages a large store near where I work." She stopped, smiled broadly, then added, "And he is, as I said, wonderful!"

Jenny and her mother were walking home from the Põltsamaa railroad station and as they approached the steps up to their door they spotted Jenny's father coming home from the other direction.

"Oh, *Isa*, there you are! Mamma said you had gone hunting. What did you bring us for our supper?"

Jenny could tell he was pleased to see her, even though he made a show of only tolerating her exuberant hug. "No luck with the hunting today," he said, spreading out his empty hands. "Maybe tomorrow I will bag a fine goose for Mamma to cook for you while you are home."

Brushing past Jenny to pull open the door, Marta muttered under her breath, "Always hunting – but never anything to show for it."

Ignoring her comment, if indeed he even heard it, the stocky man continued, "Tell me all about your life as an independent woman, daughter. How is your apartment? Do you feel safe there?"

Jenny patiently answered her father's questions. She knew he was concerned about her going out on her own in the big city. It was bad enough for him when she was staying with Aunt Frieda but now that she was living in her own apartment, he was especially uneasy. "My place is perfect, *Isa*. And very safe. I bicycle to work very easily, too."

Marta, busying herself helping Jenny put away her small travel case, said, "Vaike will be home from school any minute now. She'll be so happy to see you. In fact, she begged Karl for permission to not go to school today so she could be here when you arrived." Sighing, she added, "Actually, I think she would be glad to have any excuse to miss classes."

"Now, Marta, don't be too hard on her. After all, our Jenny is a hard act to follow. So industrious, and such a good girl," Karl admonished.

Jenny groaned a little but kept smiling. *Isa will always think of me as his little girl. Maybe I shouldn't mention my Osvald to him just yet.*

Vaike burst into the room full of hugs and questions about the apartment in the city and the new job. "I admit it, Jenny. I am so jealous of you. I can't wait until I'm out of school too. It all sounds so glamorous!"

"Now, Vaike, don't be in too big a hurry. Remember, I had to go to all my classes and study and work hard in school. Just be patient and it will all come together for you, too, I'm sure."

Vaike nodded, only half listening, and quickly turned the conversation back to her own life and activities.

****

When the family sat down to supper that evening, the conversation eventually turned to the recently growing Russian presence in Estonia.

The family knew only rumors, because when the Russians took over the Baltic States, they had quickly established a climate of neighbors being encouraged ... or even coerced ... to tell on neighbors, and the citizens soon learned to keep careful silence except with most trusted friends.

"Those Russians! Those damned Russians," Karl exploded. "We finally broke free from them – from everyone – and won our independence twenty years ago. We fought for it, we won it, and we deserve it. And now here they are, coming back into *our* country and announcing that we are now the 'Estonia Soviet Socialist Republic.'" He exaggerated his phrasing, making his displeasure even more clear.

"Now, now, Karl. I heard that the Russians have promised that nothing will really change. They said we can still continue our own government; that it is just a matter of helping protect us from the threat of invasion from other powerful countries." Marta kept her voice calm and looked her husband directly in the eye, a silent signal for him to keep his voice down.

"Yes," Vaike spoke up. "Besides, *Isa*, it can't be that bad. Our lives seem to go on just as before."

"Here, maybe. In our small village far away from the capitol. But I'm telling you now, no matter what they say, no matter what they want us to believe, our lives are going to change."

"Hush, Karl," soothed Marta. "Tonight we are all here together at our table, our girls are both here with us, and we *will* have a nice meal."

Karl started to object, but when he looked around the table at his daughters' faces, he realized he wasn't getting anywhere with his tirade. Vaike looked bored, Marta was obviously aggravated with him, and his Jenny seemed stunned.

"Oh, very well," he conceded. More quietly, he added, "But I'm right. Mark my words. None of you can begin to understand how bad things can get for us under the Bolsheviks – even here in quiet little Põltsamaa."

Later, sitting on her bed in the room she and Vaike had shared throughout their childhoods, Jenny confided to her younger sister what she had not yet had the courage to tell her father.

"Oh, Vaike! He is so gorgeous! He has the most beautiful eyes."

"What's his name? You haven't told me his name." Vaike was practically wriggling with the suspense.

"Osvald Laumets." Jenny loved the way his name felt in her mouth; almost like a tangible thing in itself. "I call him Oss. He tells me I'm the only person – except for one of his old aunts – that he allows to call him that."

"Are you seeing him? Officially 'going out,' I mean."

"Yes. We are. He started just talking to me on the sidewalk when I passed his store at first, then he finally asked me to go to the theater with him and a couple of his friends, and it has just kept going from there.

"Oh ... the theater! Was it wonderful? It must be so exciting to live in Tallinn and go to the theater whenever you want. Not like being stuck here."

"It is exciting," agreed Jenny. "A little scary though, too. Especially if what *Isa* says is right. But really, when I'm with Oss it is exciting no matter where we go or what we do." Jenny could feel her lips spreading into a big smile. "He is so handsome, too,

Flight to Freedom

Vaike. Very tall and strong. And I think he really adores me," she added softly, glad that their bedroom was dark, lighted only by a glow from the moonlight outside the window. She knew she was blushing and if her sister could have seen it, there would never be any end to the teasing.

The sisters, although very different in personality, had no trouble talking together almost all night, taking care to be quiet so as not to disturb their sleeping parents. For a change, the normally reserved Jenny did almost all the talking, as the normally vivacious Vaike was eager to hear everything about the city, about how it felt to be "grown up," and especially how it felt to have a real suitor. Jenny was so full of her plans and dreams she couldn't have stopped talking if she had tried.

Secretly, Vaike considered her own dreams to be much grander than her sister's, but still she wanted to soak up as much information as she could, so she would be ready when her turn came to go out into the big, wonderful world.

****

"Oh, Oss, my father has given us his blessing." Jenny's face clearly showed her pleasure at this bit of news.

"That is good news," the sturdy young man responded. "I know how important that must be for you." He pulled her closer, in a great hug. Then, putting his hands on her shoulders and straightening his arms, he held Jenny so that he could look into her eyes. "But you know ... I would have married you anyway."

Jenny smiled, then tried to rearrange her face into a more stern expression. Giving up that effort, however, she pulled away and began to dance around the room. "He has promised to help us – financially, I mean. He asked me if we would rather have a gift of money – or a big church wedding."

"And what did we choose?"

"I chose the big wedding, Oss. Our church is gorgeous, and our wedding will be grand. I will have the perfect dress, and we can invite all our friends and family ... " She stopped twirling, and reached out for his hand. "That is, if it's all right with you. It is, isn't it? Oh, I hope you agree. But if you don't, it ... "

Osvald laughed his big hearty laugh that Jenny so loved. "Of course, of course, my darling. Whatever makes you happy." He pulled her back close to his chest. "And I will be the proudest man in the world to stand beside my beautiful bride in her beautiful church."

4

The next time Jenny traveled to Põltsamaa from Tallinn for one of her rare visits, she found her family discussing the big picnic that was going to be held that afternoon on the town castle grounds.

"It's to celebrate the coming of the Russians," Karl explained, wryly.

"But, *Isa*, I thought you would be the last person to celebrate that. You said ..."

"Hush, daughter. We must go."

"Oh! Oh, *Isa*, what has changed? What has happened?" Jenny looked from her father's face to her mother's, and back again.

"Several of our neighbors have 'disappeared.'"

Jenny leaned back, stunned.

Her father continued, in an even lower voice, "You remember the Tooming family? I think their son Tiiu was a few years behind you in school."

"Yes, I remember them. He has a younger sister, too. I think her name is Inge ... or maybe Helgi. Yes, that's it. Helgi. Why?"

Karl lowered his voice, looking carefully about the room. "That family is gone. All except Tiiu."

"Gone?" Jenny's heard her own voice go up, getting almost shrill. "What do you mean, *gone*?"

"Shh. Shh. They were taken away. The boy was away from the house when the soldiers came, or he would be gone too."

"Where? Why?" This time Jenny kept her voice low. She could feel her throat tightening; she couldn't have spoken loudly anyway.

"Probably Siberia. Because Mr. Tooming had the largest farm in the area."

"Because he ... ? What? I don't understand, *Isa.* What is wrong with that?"

"Because to the Communists, that is a crime. They insist that all farmers belong to the collective; all work the same and supposedly share the same. But the farmers don't get the same share. The government gets it. And the government wants the best."

"What will the family do in Siberia? Helgi is still a child!"

"Nobody knows. No one has ever come back." Karl straightened his back, only just realizing that he had been practically crouching while he spoke. "So, anyway, daughter," now he spoke clearly and more loudly, raising his head so his voice would carry, "we will go and celebrate!"

It seemed that the whole village was gathered on the commons; as well it might have been. In spite of the presence of the Russian soldiers ... in fact, because of it ... every single citizen made a point to be seen participating in the many cheers and toasts.

As the evening wore on, everyone began to relax a bit. The women of the Rissman family found a place to spread their blankets on the grass along with their friends and neighbors. There was much they wanted to say, but they all knew well which subjects to avoid.

The other women began to make a fuss over Jenny, congratulating her on her engagement. "Have you set a date?" Mrs. Tampuu, from next door, asked.

"Yes. We have it set for December 19th. We want it before Christmas," Jenny explained. "We are going to have it here at St. Nicholas' Church," she continued, gesturing toward the imposing stone steeple reaching up from the nearby castle wall. "*Isa* asked me if I wanted a big wedding or would we rather have the *kroons*. I am so excited! I chose the big wedding; it is going to be just like I have always dreamed about."

All the women nodded silently; they all knew they could not say aloud what they were all thinking. They were acutely aware that the communists were shutting down all the churches in Estonia.

Marta and her daughters barely noticed when Karl strolled by where they were sitting and announced that since he had done his duty and made his appearance at the picnic, he was going to leave. "I'm going to go hunting. I will meet you at home later," he said casually.

The women continued to talk, enjoying the food, music and entertainment provided for them. It was several hours later when they first noticed a commotion at the far end of the commons.

It was Jenny who got up from the group and went over to see what was happening. She realized a group of her neighbors were carrying what seemed to be an injured man out of the surrounding forest, and she pressed closer to see if it might be someone she knew. It was. It was her father, and he was dead.

Karl Rissman was laid to rest in the heavily wooded cemetery at the edge of town. The spot was marked with a simple wooden marker.

The following evening, after the large gathering of friends and family had finally left, Marta and her daughters alone together, sat around the kitchen table tired and drained after their ordeal.

"We are calling it a "hunting accident," Marta said suddenly.

Her daughters looked at her in silence, wondering at this unexpected statement.

"But we don't really know what happened." She looked down at her hands, which were clutched together in her lap. "He had been spending a lot of time out of the house lately. He said he was hunting, but ... he never brought home any game." She lapsed again into silence.

"Then what ... " Jenny started to ask, then stopped when she really looked at her mother's face. She was shocked to realize that the tears she saw there seemed to be from anger as much as from sorrow.

5

B ack in Tallinn, Jenny's life continued as normal; or, at least, as normal as possible considering she had graduated from business school, started a new job, moved into her own apartment, begun planning her wedding, and lost her father, all within the last few months.

As summer cooled into autumn, and evening shadows grew longer, the Russian presence loomed larger.

Before the wedding arrangements could be completed, Jenny received word from home that her church, her beautiful, big St. Nicholas' Lutheran Church, had been closed by the Soviets. Built into the town's castle walls, the building dated back to the early 1300's. The sturdy, stone structure with its soaring steeple had been a reassuring presence for Jenny her entire life. It was where she had been baptized in 1923.

"What does this mean for us, Oss?"

"Don't worry, my Jenny. We will still have our wedding; it just will have to be somewhere else. We will be just as married, you know."

"The Russians, I mean." Jenny touched his shoulder, wanting reassurance that everything would really be all right. "The things they are doing, the stories I hear ..."

"War is never easy, Jenny. There are many people who have been and will be affected by this one. But if you and I can just keep our heads down, do our jobs, and above all avoid any political discussions, we should be just fine."

Jenny allowed herself to be mollified. After all, her Oss was six years older than she, and much more experienced in the ways of the world. He had a responsible position at the shop, he loved her, and he would take care of her always.

Because she had a naturally sunny heart, Jenny focused on the joyful things; her newfound love for the steady, reliable, yet dashing Osvald, their friends, and rearranging the details for her upcoming marriage.

The December 19, 1940, wedding, drastically curtailed in scope, was a lovely affair, even though the young couple exchanged vows and matching thin gold wedding bands in front of a justice of the peace in a small office in the city instead of in the grand, soaring church in her hometown.

Jenny was pleased beyond measure to have the support of her family; Vaike came from Põltsamaa with Jenny's cousin Karl Lõuke. Karl stood up for her in place of her father, and Vaike was her maid of honor. Of course her Aunt Frieda and Uncle Ants were there for her, too. The entire group went out for a celebration dinner and managed to push the shadow of the rapidly worsening political climate to the very back of their minds.

****

After the holidays the young couple fell into a comfortable routine. As newlyweds, they were focused on creating their own new life together, and both were determined to have it be a happy life. They were determined to avoid any conflicts.

The only disappointment was Jenny's lingering feeling of fatigue. Several mornings in a row she felt she could barely drag herself out of bed to go to fix breakfast for Oss, much less ride her bicycle to her own job at the insurance office.

"Oss, Do you mind terribly if we have a simple supper tonight? I really am too tired to go to the theater after all."

"My Jenny, of course I don't mind. But are you sure you're all right? I don't like to see you not feeling well."

"I'm sure it's nothing. After all, I've had a great deal going on in my life for the last several months. I'm sure it's just a reaction to all of that. I'll be fine tomorrow."

****

But she wasn't fine the next day, or the next. Finally she agreed to see a doctor.

"What? I'm sorry; I must have misunderstood." Jenny felt stunned.

"Yes, Mrs. Laumets," the doctor repeated, "I am happy to inform you that are, indeed, pregnant."

"That can't be right. I can't be pregnant. It's too soon, we agreed to wait ... "

"Nonetheless, that is the case. I think you can expect your baby to be born around the first of October."

When Jenny started once more to protest, the doctor said sternly, "Who is the doctor here? You? Or me?

She hurried home to tell Oss the good news. *Of course it's good news. It is good news, isn't it?*

Oss was thrilled, in spite of Jenny's fretting. "Why Jenny, this is wonderful!" he beamed.

"But it's too soon," she protested, dropping into the nearest chair. "We talked about this; everything is too uncertain ... we agreed that we didn't want to start our family just yet."

"But, my Jenny, it would seem that is exactly what we are doing. So we will make the best of it." He swooped down, plucked her from the chair, and danced her around the room. "Besides, I'm happy to know that is why you've been feeling so tired. I was beginning to worry that you were finding me to be a difficult husband."

"Of course not! You're never difficult – I'm happy every day just knowing you are really mine." She smiled into his face. "I'm the one who has been difficult. But the doctor assured me that I will soon get my energy back."

She put her hand on his chest and gently pushed him away. "Speaking of that, I completely forgot to stop by the market on my way home. Now I have nothing to prepare for your supper."

"That is not a problem. I will take you out for dinner tonight to celebrate." Then Oss stopped and looked more closely into his wife's face. "Or, I can go to the market instead while you take a short nap."

"Yes, thank you, that would be wonderful," she said, already headed toward the sofa with a pillow in her hand.

****

Sure enough, soon Jenny not only began to feel better, but had a great burst of energy. She felt strong, and confident, and ready for this baby. She knew her husband would take good care of both of them, and she was thrilled that they would have their very own family. Everything was going to be just perfect.

Now she could enjoy going out with Oss again, just the two of them or with their friends. Going to the theatre became of their favorite pastimes. One night, on their way home after a lovely evening, Jenny mused, "The heroine's name was unusual, but I loved the way it sounded. *Küllike*. Do you like it?" When her husband nodded, she set her shoulders and announced, "Then it's settled. If our baby is a girl, we will name her Küllike."

6

In spite of the constant presence of armed Russian soldiers on every street corner in Tallinn, Jenny and Oss were determined to avoid trouble and to make their own happiness.

Then, one evening Jenny was humming to herself as she worked in their small kitchen, chopping mushrooms and onions for a casserole for her husband's evening meal. When she heard him come into the room, she turned with a broad smile. "Look, Oss. I found your favorite mushrooms at the market, and I'm making *seenevorm* ... "

She froze in place, with her vegetable knife held in the air, as soon as she saw his face. "What is it? What's wrong?"

Oss just stood there, looking down at an official-looking document he was holding in both hands. Slowly he raised his eyes to meet hers. She could clearly read there fear and pain and anger and sadness. They stood there for a dozen heartbeats, each afraid to move. "I've been conscripted," he said, almost whispering. "I have to report to the train station tomorrow morning at 10 o'clock."

Suddenly Jenny was galvanized into action. She flew to his side, jerking the paper from his hand but refusing to look at it. "No! No no no no!" She kept repeating the word, gradually lowering her voice until it was almost inaudible.

Oss put his arms out and gathered the small, sobbing figure into a warm hug. They remained standing there in silence, clinging not only to each other but to their future, their dreams, the laughter of their unborn child.

Supper was forgotten, the chopped mushrooms and onions shriveling on the counter next to the sauté pan which held an unmelted lump of butter.

Throughout the night, the young couple alternately huddled together on their small brown sofa and paced the floor of the apartment. Jenny wanted desperately to understand what all their options were. Oss patiently explained, over and over, that there were no options.

"I thought your last birthday put you above the cutoff age for the draft." Jenny said, hopefully.

"That's right. But they've just expanded the eligible age limits ... by nine years. Younger and older, we all have to join."

"How can they do that?"

"The Soviet machine can do anything they want." Bitterness gave his voice a distinct edge. "And what they want is for every last able bodied man in Estonia to belong to them. Germany is gaining strength and if they should gain control of Estonia, the Russians don't want to leave anything here that they might use. Apparently that includes all able bodied men."

Jenny continued to protest, grasping at every idea, every possibility.

"But what, what would happen if you simply didn't report?"

"They would come get me, and I would immediately be sent to a prison camp. Probably in Siberia." He sighed. "I have to go, Jenny."

"We're not even Russian, Oss. They just came in here and took over. We don't want to fight their wars for them!"

"Ah, but we are part of the Soviet Socialist Republic now, don't you see? When they annexed us, as far as they are concerned, all Estonians became Russians."

Jenny took a jagged breath. "What if you left and they couldn't find you? I've overheard conversations at the office about the *Forest Brothers*, or whatever those rebels are called. They're men like you who've banded together to resist the Soviets. You could leave now ... right now ... tonight ... and join them." She felt her hands tightening into fists. "I would rather have you fighting for our own country than fighting for the communists!" Jenny had no more tears; anger was taking over and she was focused on the problem at hand, willing to make any sacrifice to keep her husband safe.

A little surprised that Jenny even knew about the resisters, Oss took both her hands in his own and squeezed them tightly. "I would be sorely tempted to do just that, if I had only myself to consider. I hate the Russians and all that they stand for. It galls me beyond measure to think I will be helping them."

Jenny brightened. "So, if I say it's all right, you'll go to the forest? I'll support you in that decision, with all my might. I'll get along without you somehow; I'm sure I can make do. My family will help me. Us," she amended, gently stroking her rounded belly.

He sighed deeply. "I can't do that, my Jenny. What you have not heard is what the Reds do to the families of the rebels. I cannot let that happen to you ... or our baby." He knew he was telling his young, pregnant wife details of a concept that she already knew with her head, but couldn't accept with her heart. He had to make her understand.

"I've heard more details than perhaps you have. The families of the rebels are being targeted. Tortured, sent to prison camps, ostensibly to extract information about the group and their location. There have been whole families killed," he added, very quietly.

Jenny lowered her eyes, letting her shoulders slump as she leaned back against the loose cushions. "Oh, of course. We can't let anything happen to our baby." Her eyes filled again with tears.

Giving herself a little shake, she sat up straight again, looking on the brighter side. "Well, at least in the army you will have food and shelter and clothing. I won't have to worry about you sleeping on the ground in the woods in the wintertime, like I would if you did join the resistance."

"You must go at once to your mother's house, of course. It's getting way too dangerous here in the capitol. You'll be safer in the countryside and your mother can help you with the baby ... " Oss stopped, unable to continue.

"Of course. I will go immediately. I can help Mamma, too. I know things must be hard for her since *Isa* ... " Jenny, too, choked on unshed tears.

"You'll be the head of our little household now, so you must hold things together for me. I will come directly to Põltsamaa for you as soon as I can."

They sat in the dark all night long, murmuring, crying softly, and consoling one another.

The next morning, Oss went through his clothing, packing what he could fit into the one valise he had been instructed to take with him. Jenny went to their big chest and dug out his heavy wool winter coat. "I know it won't fit in the bag, but you'll need it this winter; maybe you can just carry it over your arm."

Oss smiled, but declined to take it. "No, the army will provide me with a uniform as soon as I get to the training camp. I'm sure that will include a coat and heavy boots, too, for that matter. Please keep it for me until I come home again."

At Tallinn's *Balti Jaam* station the next morning, Oss and Jenny stood packed in a crowd composed mostly of young men, all conscripts on their way to join the Red Army, and their parents, spouses or girlfriends. The mood was generally subdued, and the cloud of uncertainly that floated over their heads seemed a tangible object.

When a uniformed officer began barking orders Oss quickly pulled off his still-shiny wedding band and pressed it into Jenny's palm. When she looked at him questioningly, he explained. "Keep this. I don't trust the men I will be with. Keep it next to your heart."

Then he was brusquely hustled off with no chance even for a last kiss, and packed onto the third of a long line of rail cars.

Jenny stood quite still in the remaining crowd, watching the tall, strong figure disappear in the crush of other reluctant draftees. In vain she watched the windows for at least one last glimpse of her husband's face. With a great hiss and a series of loud metallic clangs, the ordinary looking train, with its extraordinary passengers, pulled away from the platform, enveloping those who remained in a thick cloud of steam.

With a start, Jenny became aware all at once of the rapidly dispersing crowd around her, the beginning of a misty rain, and ... her baby, kicking inside her belly.

Placing one palm protectively on the front of her skirt, she pressed a little, pleased beyond measure when she felt the baby kick against it. All the way back to the apartment, Jenny kept up a silent, internal communication, patting and humming softly. *I will be strong. I can do this. I will protect you and keep you safe, little one, so you can meet your Isa one day.*

When she realized she was still gripping Oss's wedding band in her other hand, she went to her dresser and rummaged through the carved wooden chest where she kept her few pieces of jewelry. Selecting a sturdy gold chain, she threaded the ring onto it and placed it carefully around her neck. Now the ring was, in fact, next to her heart.

7

As quickly and efficiently as she could, Jenny packed up her most important belongings and prepared to move from Tallinn back to her childhood home to be with her mother and sister.

Jenny was lucky to find a friend of her family who was leaving right away to drive to Põltsamaa. He helped her load her few belongings onto the back of his small, aged truck, and they were on their way as quickly as possible.

The trip home was arduous and nerve wracking. The Germans had begun a strong push into Estonia from the west, intent on seizing control of the Baltic States; and the now retreating Russians were implementing their "scorched earth" policy with a vengeance, destroying many of the historic old buildings in Tallinn and Tartu.

As soon as Jenny and her friend came within view of the Põltsamaa castle, they were saddened to see that the beautiful ancient church had been almost totally destroyed.

****

By the time Jenny was safely back in her mother's home, her family and neighbors were celebrating their salvation by the Germans, who were well on their way to claiming Estonia for their own.

When the Nazis "liberated" Estonia from the Soviet repression, the mood of the population was at first jubilant; initially the saviors were welcomed with boundless relief. But the citizens soon found that there was a dark side, a very dark side, to the new leader's plans for their small country.

They were not to be truly liberated; instead, they had now been incorporated into the German province of Ostland.

However, in little Põltsamaa, the townspeople discovered that their new "masters" were less aggressive in pursuing their goals than the Bolsheviks had been, so they were able to adapt to the new situation.

Vaike peppered her older sister with questions, eager to hear all the latest news from the big city. "Nothing changes here in little old Põltsamaa," she groused one sunny afternoon as they were hanging the week's laundry on the line.

Jenny whirled to face Vaike. "Do not ever complain again about 'nothing ever happens here.' Sure, a lot's happened in Tallinn - a *lot* - and none of it is good. The soldiers are everywhere, people are disappearing, and all the young men – *my* young man included – have been taken away.

"I've heard that it wasn't even legal for the Red Army to take him. Stalin did not have the right by International Treaty to change the age limits for conscription. But they took him anyway. And they haven't let him even write to me! I haven't heard one single word. None of the other wives have, either. What we do hear is rumors."

Jenny stopped to take a breath, brushing a curl off her heated face with a worried sigh. "And the rumors – they are too awful to believe – too awful to even think about." She let herself slump to the ground, leaning against the laundry basket for support.

Vaike was stunned. Finally she dropped down beside Jenny and hugged her awkwardly. "Oh, Jen, I'm so sorry. I've been so stupid. I didn't think ..."

"That's it, of course. You didn't think. If something doesn't happen right in front of your face you don't even give it a thought."

Stung, Vaike withdrew her arm and sat back on her heels. After a moment she leaned forward, gently kissing Jenny's forehead. "I'm sorry," she repeated. "I've been blind. I wanted everything to just go back to normal. I hate this war. I hated everything about it as soon as I heard that our *Eesti* had been 'annexed' by the Russians."

She took a deep breath and continued, more slowly now, "But I didn't really realize. I see that now. You've been so brave and stoic, and I just saw what I wanted to see."

Sniffling, Jenny reached out and pulled Vaike into a proper, strong hug, not letting go even as they struggled back to their feet.

"I know, I know. I'm sorry too. You didn't deserve that. I didn't understand either, not really, not until they took Oss. Now, let's finish getting this laundry on the line before it gets dark."

****

Jenny almost immediately found a job, as a typist in an insurance agency in town. It kept her busy, and she felt she was making a real contribution to the upkeep of her mother's household. She knew that soon enough, when her baby was born, she would be leaning on Marta for support.

8

"Mamma, Mamma, wake up." Jenny gently shook her sleeping mother's shoulder.

Marta sat up almost immediately. "What is it? Is it time?"

This was not the first time Jenny had felt contractions, but she was sure that this time they were the real thing. "Yes. I've been awake for several hours, and now the pains are getting much stronger."

Marta clambered out of bed, going first to wake Vaike and send her to fetch the doctor.

"Mamma, don't ask the doctor to come here. I want to go to the hospital."

"Shh, shh. You know the hospitals are full now, taking care of the injured soldiers."

"I know, but if the Germans came to save us from the Russians, shouldn't they ... ?"

"Shh, shh, Jenny. Keep your voice down." Marta looked over her shoulder. "They didn't come to save us. They came here because we are on their way to conquer Russia. We're not significant to them."

"But, Mamma, I don't want to have my baby at home."

"You'll be fine. The doctor will come soon and he will take care of you here just like you were in the hospital."

"But what if something goes wrong?" Jenny did not want to be afraid; she wanted to be brave and strong. But with the next powerful, painful cramp she could feel her courage rapidly ebbing away.

Vaike returned, not with a doctor but with a message. "All the doctors and nurses are too busy caring for the soldiers. They told me to tell you, 'Having a baby is easy. You'll be fine.'"

Marta quickly reassured Jenny that nothing would go wrong, putting on her best stern face as she prepared to deliver her first grandchild.

The night seemed to drag on forever, but even when the hazy autumn sun was well up in the sky, Jenny was still in intense labor, her damp hair clinging to her dripping forehead.

Vaike stayed by her side, periodically patting her sister's forehead with a damp cloth, getting up from her uncomfortable position only to replace and refresh the cool water in the heavy earthenware bowl she held in her lap.

"Here, let me unclasp your necklace, it must be uncomfortable to have it sticking to your sweaty skin like that," Vaike offered, reaching toward Jenny.

"No, don't. I want to keep it on. I must keep it on. I promised Oss." Jenny shrank back, wrapping her fingers tightly around the ring that hung there. "Especially now, I need to know it's right here," she explained.

Finally, as the long October day faded back into nighttime darkness, Jenny's baby made her appearance. A big, healthy, squalling infant, she instantly won her mother's heart.

"Welcome, my little Küllike," Jenny murmured, touching the infants' face softly, aware that the tears rolling down her own cheeks were from both joy and sadness ... as well as just plain exhaustion.

9

One day the mailman delivered a postcard for Jenny and he said it was from Oss! She squeezed her baby even more tightly to her bosom with one hand as she reached out the other, murmuring, "Oh, my baby, it's from your *Isa*! Your very own father! I knew he would write. Oh, he will love you so much."

She let her eyes linger over the details on the address side of the card, savoring the closeness she felt just seeing her name, her *married* name, written in his so familiar handwriting.

Then she froze. It was addressed to their apartment in Tallinn. *That's strange. He knew I would be leaving immediately to come home to Põltsamaa.* Then she saw the date - July 29, 1941 – the very day he had been taken away!

She swayed, almost falling against the postman, who had remained beside her when he saw her face lose all its color.

Almost numbly, Jenny continued to peruse the face of the card, and noticed that it had been postmarked twice: once in Tallinn and the second time in Põltsamaa. Slowly, she turned it over in her hand and read aloud, with quivering lips:

> *Dearest Wife.*
> *Traveling along rapidly. The men seem happy, always singing. I don't have the same feeling. I'm sad from the last vision of you at the train station, but try to understand that we have to go along with everything – as you saw how we were herded on the train. Now we have stopped at Aeguiidus.*
>
> *Oss*

She turned to the postman. "I don't understand. Why did it take so long to get to me?"

"Mrs. Laumets, apparently this card was pushed out of a slot on the train. A citizen of Aeguiidus found it on the ground beside the railroad track, and he kindly took it to the post office there. Once it arrived in Tallinn, of course, there was no Mrs. Laumets at that address."

Marta heard voices, and came outside to join them, wiping her hands on her apron. She saw Jenny's face and hurried over to silently offer her support.

The postman looked from one distraught face to the other, nodded to Marta, and continued, "And you realize that the mail service was severely disrupted when the Russians retreated and practically destroyed the city as they left. Not to mention the rail lines and bridges and most of the city of Tartu ..." his voice trailed off.

****

As soon as Jenny walked into the house, she sought her bed. She lay face down on top of the covers and immediately fell in to a deep sleep, not waking until mid-morning of the next day.

Although she had no appetite, she allowed her mother to persuade her to join her at the kitchen table.

"I'm sure this is a good thing, Jenny," Marta crooned. "Now you have heard from Oss, and I'm sure there must be more cards and letters still out there. Now you know he is all right."

"No. Oh, no, Mamma. Oss is *not* all right. This just confirms the rumors – they've truly taken him away. If they wouldn't let him even mail a note to his wife, if he had to slip it off the train, he really has been taken. He was going through Aeguiidus! That is on the way to Russia ... "

Finally running out of steam, Jenny let her head drop forward, unconsciously reaching for the gold ring on its chain. When her fingers touched the metal, her hand jerked away.

"What?" Marta asked, concerned.

"The ring. Oss's ring. It's so cold."

10

One evening after Jenny had nursed the baby and put her down for the night in her little wooden crib, tucking the small quilted blanket under her chin and kissing her tenderly on her soft warm forehead, Marta brought up a subject she had been thinking about for some time. "Jenny," she began, "now that Küllike has been almost totally weaned, how would you feel about looking for a job? I could certainly care for her during the daytime."

Jenny sat down beside her mother on their old sofa. Secretly she was quite pleased at the suggestion. It was clear that Marta was an excellent caregiver, and that she loved the baby as much – well, almost as much – as

Jenny did. And Jenny did so want to get back out into the world beyond their front door.

"I was thinking the same thing, Mamma. In fact, just today at the market, Madis Tamm mentioned that the police dispatchers' office is looking for secretarial help."

"Oh, that would be ideal for you. It would be close enough to walk, and you could even come home for lunch."

The baby thrived under her *vanaema*'s care, and the four females in the small extended family managed to keep their lives reasonably uneventful for several years.

****

The winds of war and the oppression of the Nazis brought deprivation and a frisson of fear to their everyday lives, but the family was careful not to make waves. The need for reticence persisted even among neighbors who had been friends for years, because the Germans, like the Russians before them, encouraged citizens to save themselves at the expense of others. The family bonded even more closely together.

****

"Ah, Jenny, there you are," Marta exclaimed, looking up from the stove, where she had been stirring a simmering pot of cut-up vegetables from their garden.

"Küllike has been asking when you would be home. I think she has something to show you."

The little girl came running into the room, her blonde hair bouncing. "Memme, Memme," she squealed, throwing herself headlong into her mother's arms. "Look what I made for you!" She proudly held up the little doll she had made from a wooden spool, twine, and several colorful beads. She had even glued on yellow "hair" made of short lengths of yarn.

"Oh, my! Now isn't she just beautiful!" Jenny took the small object, holding it up to the light and looking at it from different angles. "Did you make this all by yourself?"

"Well, maybe Mamma helped a little bit."

Jenny laughed. "Thank you, my darling." She tried to hand it back to Küllike, but the little girl put her hands behind her back, stubbornly refusing to take it.

"No, Memme. I made her for you," she said earnestly. "Just for you!"

Jenny encircled the doll and her daughter with both arms. "I know; and I love her. You know what I think? I think she would love to stay with you, though. So she won't be lonely while I'm at work. Look – she just fits in your pocket – there. How's that?

Patting the pocket on her blue skirt, the little girl announced, "That's just perfect."

"What did you name her?"

"*You* should name her, Memme."

"All right. I know. I'll call her ... Evie. How about that? Evie means *life*." Her voice became wistful. *"Life."*

Marilyn Smith Neilans   49

11

"Mamma! Come! We must go. Now!" The young woman, having awakened in the very early morning to the steadily increasing rumbling of Russian tanks, felt fear but not panic. She knew now what she must do to protect her young daughter, her mother, and herself and she was prepared to move heaven and earth to do so.

The evening before, Jenny had told her mother that one of her co-workers at the Põltsamaa Police station had pulled her aside, whispering urgently: "The Germans are losing the war. All the Germans at the station have been ordered to retreat. The borders are being closed. You must come with us; the Russians are coming back ... with a vengeance! We will leave soon; be ready."

The older woman had demurred, saying noncommittally, "Perhaps we should go, but not yet, not yet. When Vaike returns from her girlfriend's house we can all talk about it."

"But Mamma, I heard that because *Isa* came to this country from Germany, even though he became an Estonian citizen, we are considered to be German!"

When her mother started to protest, Jenny continued even more urgently, "And because I work at the station, our names will be marked by the Russians; we will be considered collaborators." She paused for just a beat. "You must know what that means.

"The officer said that we can go with them. But we must pack tonight, this very evening, and be ready. Don't you see?" Even as she made her plea, Jenny could see by her mother's firmly set chin that she would not prevail in this discussion, at least not until her younger sister's return.

"It will be okay, Jenny." Marta had continued. "We will sleep now, and there will be time to pack in the morning."

Now there was no more time. Jenny grabbed her suitcase, throwing into it anything she could put her hands on, then doing the same for her mother's belongings. Stooping awkwardly with the bag banging her thigh, she lifted Küllike with her other hand, cradling her sleepy head against her neck and whispering reassuring words she herself did not believe. "Shh, shh, my baby. Everything will be all right. Sleep again, my darling."

Jenny jerked open the heavy door and was relieved beyond measure to see the familiar big white and blue police truck already turning into their back alley. "Mamma!" she repeated, propping the door open with her foot.

"I'm coming, I'm coming." Marta was grasping her own small bag but rather than moving, she stood still, looking about distractedly. "But, Jenny, Vaike is not home yet. Where can she be? We must wait for her."

"Mamma, she will have to find us later. We have to go now." Jenny was already going out the door, passing her bag to the young man who had bounded up the steps to help her. She turned, and with her now-free hand pulled her mother's elbow, almost dragging her down to the alley. Their door swung shut behind them, with an achingly final bang.

Several hands reached down and literally lifted all three of them into the open truck bed, the other passengers' bodies shifting to make room. Very few words were spoken; all were intensely aware of the approaching tanks. The truck jolted into motion before

Jenny, with Küllike still held snugly under her chin, had found her balance. She fell the last few inches, but only wedged more tightly among the others.

Little Küllike had awakened and looked around at all the strangers. She seemed as though ready to cry, then turned her head up to look into her mother's face. She evidently drew comfort from the familiar blue eyed gaze, for she immediately snuggled deeper into the comforting embrace and remained quiet. She did not, however, loosen for an instant her strong grasp around Jenny's neck.

As the roar of the dreaded tanks dwindled behind them, Jenny's pounding heart slowed just a bit. At some point she noticed that another big truck from the police department had joined them in their flight. Somehow she felt safer because they were there, even though she fully realized that the Russians, with their tanks and heavy weapons, could easily overpower this small group of refugees with their families, friends and coworkers.

By the very act of fleeing, every single person in their ragtag group had as much as declared themselves enemies of the Soviet state; Jenny knew she and her family now faced certain death or deportation. And deportation meant Siberia ... which also meant death.

Willing herself not to dwell on the great gaping void that was to be her future – and her daughter's, and her mother's - Jenny finally allowed herself to fall into a half doze, with her cheek bumping against her daughter's soft curls.

Eventually, the heavy vehicle slowed, then pulled off the road and stopped in an area of dense foliage. Stretching and softly murmuring to each other, looking about them with wide, alert eyes, the passengers climbed stiffly out of the back of the truck, jumping or falling to the ground. They broke into small groups, stretching while walking around to relieve their cramped and spasming muscles. Everyone was careful not to stray too far from the perceived safety offered by the big trucks.

Jenny and her family had brought a little food, as had the others, and soon loaves of hard bread, bits of cheese and canteens of water were being passed around. Sinking down onto the soft green undergrowth, Jenny gratefully accepted the offering, being careful to take only small morsels for Küllike and herself before passing the loaves and chunks of cheese on to Marta, who in turn passed them on to the next person.

"Where are we going? Where will we be safe?" Marta asked quietly, with a sideways look at her granddaughter, not wanting to distress the child snuggled against Jenny's thigh, quietly playing with the tiny doll they'd named Evie. Bedraggled and by now quite bald, the handmade toy was still much beloved, and apparently possessed the power to calm the little girl in spite of the turmoil surrounding them.

"We won't be safe anywhere in Estonia if the Russians continue to force the Germans to retreat." Jenny tried to suppress a quavering sigh. "We'll have to try to find a ship to take us away."

"Oh, Jenny! I've never been on a boat before. I can't swim! None of us can swim … "

"Hush, Mamma, it'll be all right." Jenny heard again her own words of assurance, again knowing how hollow they sounded; yet how important it was for her to speak them.

"I think we're going to Pärnu, at the coast." Jenny whispered. "My friends at the station said only that they planned to go as far away from the Russians as possible. The German Army is retreating, and ceding us back to the Communists." Jenny sighed a deep, sad, worried sigh. "We can only hope that they will let us join them on a troop ship headed for Germany."

At almost three years of age, little Küllike was old enough to respond to her mother's and grandmother's whispered commands to stay quiet and to be still, and yet, thankfully, still young enough to need more hours of sleep than the adults.

Jenny placed her suitcase on the long grasses, then lay with her head resting upon it; both to achieve some sort of comfort for her exhausted body, and also to keep her few belongings close for safekeeping. Her mother lay beside her, and they cradled little Küllike between them. Jenny spread Oss's heavy woolen coat over all three of them for an imperfect warmth as they tried to sleep in the chill night air.

She slept only fitfully. Every time she awoke she worried about her future and her daughter's, and of course her sister's, too. *Where was Vaike?* Jenny felt a flare up of anger, just for a moment. Vaike had told their mother that she was going to a girlfriend's house for the evening. *But I'll bet anything that she is out with that boy!*

She immediately squelched her annoyance. *Oh please God, keep her safe. Please keep all of us safe.*

She hugged her little girl even more tightly. With her free hand, she unconsciously clasped the thin gold band at her neck.

****

The hard, jouncing trip through the forests of western Estonia seemed to never end. The entire group of refugees, exhausted, hungry, and almost numb with fright, ceased speaking entirely, and concentrated all their efforts on simply existing. They no longer even looked over their shoulders, even though the threat of being captured never lessened.

The Pärnu River came into sight beside the road and the trucks followed it to Pärnu Bay on the Gulf of Riga on the Baltic Sea. When the group finally reached the city, the passengers were overwhelmed by the bustle and noise of the busy port. The drivers managed to navigate through the throngs of men and women desperate to escape the country they had loved so well.

"I think we must be almost to the docks," Jenny said to her mother in a low voice, craning her neck to see past the others' heads.

Marta, seated at the rear of the truck, leaned over to get a better view. When she realized that the huge structure that towered over her head was the side of the troop ship, she tipped her head back, drew in a great breath with an audible gasp, and finally managed to say only, "Oh my."

Jenny jostled a little for a better position, and then she, too, raised her eyes up and up. Awed, she could say nothing. She had seen ships at the docks in Tallinn, but only from a distance; never from this close. She had had no idea they were this imposing. She silently reached for her mother's hand while drawing little Küllike closer.

Soon the three of them were helped down from the bed of the truck and they followed the crowd up the swaying gangway and onto the deck of the already packed ship. Even though every single person was filled with fear, they managed to maintain order, each eventually finding an area large enough to allow them to sit and stretch out.

More quickly than Jenny and Marta would have believed possible, the ship's lines were cast and the great vessel chugged out on its way to cross the Baltic Sea, seeking safety and shelter in its homeland, Germany.

As soon as the ship was well away from the port and in the open sea, Jenny sighed deeply, only then realizing that she had been practically holding her breath for the last few days. "We're on our way, Mamma," she said, speaking loudly now so she could be heard over the ships engines' rumblings.

"Yes, but on our way to *where*?" queried Marta.

"Germany, I'm sure," Jenny answered.

"No, what I really mean is, on our way to *what*." Marta clarified. "What sort of place are we going to? What will become of us? And what will Vaike do?" The older woman's eyes filled, finally, with tears she had not allowed herself to shed. "Oh, my poor Vaike," she mourned.

Almost as soon as they entered open water, the ship began to roll relentlessly, and many of the passengers found themselves staggering to the rail to retch into the sea; some couldn't reach the railing, but the others simply moved out of the way, trying to quell their own stomach upsets.

Eventually the wind changed, the waves calmed, and everyone could settle down for another interminable period of waiting. Occasionally hard rolls and pieces of beef jerky were passed around, each person taking only what he or she needed and then sharing the rest.

Jenny looked up at the finally blue sky, and saw a small flock of cranes flying across the bow of the ship. She stood transfixed, watching them until their silhouettes disappeared in the distance. "*Teele, teele, kurekesed ule metsa maa ...*"she heard herself singing softly to herself. "Go, go dear cranes, over forests, over land ..." *They are going away, far away ... like we are.* The sight of the familiar birds following their ages-old path to their wintering grounds gave her a feeling of hope. *Perhaps we will be home again too, by the time they return in the spring.* She knew that would not happen, but her heart felt a tiny bit lighter, just the same.

****

Often, when Küllike was napping with Marta in the crowded berth, Jenny made her way through the crowd, stopping to talk with passengers from other parts of the country; she was hungry for both hard news and for speculation about the war; what had happened, what was happening, and what might happen next.

On deck, the people were a little more open and less guarded in their conversation than they had been at home. Now they were not so worried that what they said would be reported, as had been the case everywhere in Estonia since the beginning of the war. Under both the Communists and the Nazis, every word spoken aloud had had to be carefully thought out; even seemingly innocent comments could possibly endanger their own or their neighbors' lives. Every single Estonian on board had been affected in one way or another by the two cruel regimes.

She knew that Marta would be interested, too, to hear all the details she could gather, so she edged closer to a group of men speaking in solemn tones.

"Did you hear?" One of the older men was saying. "The Russians sank the "Moero."

"Wasn't that a Red Cross ship?"

"Aren't hospital ships supposed to be protected from any attacks?"

A woman's voice rose above the others. "Are you sure it was the *Moero*?"

"That's what I heard the crew say."

"How? Where? When?"

"Last week. The Russians used aerial torpedoes ... they bombed it almost as soon as the ship had left the dock in Tallinn ...

"*After* it had left the dock ... that means ... it was loaded ... with refugees!"

Flight to Freedom

"Yes. They say there were three thousand souls lost."

"My cousins in Tallinn were going to be on that ship!"

The comments came too fast; voices interrupted each other, growing higher and shriller as the crowd jostled and gasped.

Jenny stopped moving; her breathing was ragged and her ears were ringing. She couldn't comprehend what she was hearing. Even though the news of the fighting throughout the course of the war had never been good, this information shocked her to her core. Not only was the number of casualties staggering, it was the demographic of the victims that hit her so hard: Estonian refugees and retreating German soldiers on board a ship bound for Germany - *just like us*, Jenny thought, as she slid slowly down to the wooden deck.

PART TWO

Germany

1944 – 1950

"Geislingen was a gentle purgatory –
a way-stop between the hell of war
and hope of tomorrow."

Priit Vesilind
Author, *The Singing Revolution*

12

Danzig loomed in the distance; a loud bustling war-torn seaport city, with no time or energy to spend on the ragged, exhausted waves of frightened refugees seeking shelter from the advancing Soviet machine.

"There, there, everything will be all right," Marta crooned to her small granddaughter.

"I want to see, too, Memme." Küllike tugged Marta's hand, pulling her toward their fellow passengers who were massing against the rail.

"Certainly. Here you go." Jenny stepped in and swooped Küllike up in her arms, holding her high enough to see over at least a few shoulders. The child was fascinated, watching the crew as they busied themselves docking the heavily loaded troop ship and tying it up to a large pier.

Marta and Jenny were watching, too, but they were more worried than fascinated.

"What happens now, my daughter?"

"I wish I knew, Mamma. We will just have to stay with the crowd." Jenny, too, was on full alert. "We've made it across the sea, and we will be safe now." *Oh, how I wish that I believed that.*

Jenny had not yet told her mother the news about the sinking of the hospital ship "Moero" and the loss of so many thousands of Estonian and German lives, or most of the other bits of bad news she had gleaned through conversations with their fellow refugees. Because Marta had stayed close to Küllike from the time they had boarded the ship in Pärnu, she knew only what Jenny had chosen to tell her, and Jenny wanted to keep it that way as much as possible.

The two women stumbled down the ramp onto German soil, each clutching their few belongings in one hand while holding one of little Küllike's hands with the other.

"Where do we go, where can we be safe, what ... ?"

"Oh, Mamma, I only know what I have heard from the others, and they really don't know, either. We've come this far; now we'll just have to continue to follow them and go where they go."

"But, Jenny ... " Marta continued.

"Mamma, I have said all I can say. Let's just be sure we don't get separated from the others." Jenny squared her shoulders, gave a little tug on her daughter's small hand, and stepped forward with a determination she certainly did not feel.

"You're right, of course," Marta agreed, finding a strength in herself that she had not truly known before.

Küllike, meanwhile, delighted with the prospect of freedom from the constraints of shipboard living, and unaware of the grim realities facing her family, was grinning merrily.

Jenny and Marta quickly realized that they had already lost all familiar faces from the ship in the huge throng, so they simply followed the flow. Jennie eventually spotted a relatively quiet corner, and the three of them sank down onto a long wooden bench with a collective sigh.

Looking around at the rag tag, exhausted, dirty group of refugees pressing into them from all sides, Marta swooped Küllike up onto her lap. "At least the floor isn't moving," she said with a wan smile.

****

Eventually, a brusque man with a Red Cross tag on his shirt ushered the small family through all the confusion and they eventually found themselves crammed aboard a train bound for Berlin.

Jenny dozed off, slumping against the stoic Marta who held Küllike tightly on her lap. She could not relax, though, because the clacking of the wheels and the hissing of the steam from the engine reminded her too vividly of the last time she had seen her husband.

The train pulled into the capital in the dark hours of the night, and the weary group, whose numbers had increased three fold over the course of the journey thus far, disembarked. They were given a bit of food and shown to a space beside the station where they could stretch out for a while.

During the darkest part of the night everyone, even though they were almost numb with exhaustion, jerked awake to the shrill wailing of air raid sirens. They were all quick to react, scrambling to their feet and following the locals into a crowded underground shelter. Citizens and refugees alike shared the cramped space without complaint.

"Oh, Jenny," Marta whispered, as if afraid the attacking aircraft might hear her words above the cacophony of the sirens, and involuntarily wincing at every blast. "Oh, Jenny," she repeated, more urgently.

"Mamma, it will be all right. We are safe in here, and soon the planes will be gone ... " but Jenny's whispered words were drowned out by the repeated blasts of bombs nearby. Dust and dirt and other small particles of debris fell from the ceiling and walls, but everyone was too afraid to even cough.

Jenny slowly became aware of a ragged noise in the room, very close by. Up to that moment she had not been aware that she ... and apparently everyone else in the room ... had been holding their breath.

Although she had seen the destruction of war in Tallinn, and then in Tartu when she made her way through that beautiful city on her way back home after Oss had been taken, and even in her own beloved Põltsamaa, where the lovely old church and much of the ancient, sturdy castle walls had been destroyed, she had never been this close to actual falling missiles.

I can't stand it any more! I've come so far from home, I've tried to be brave, Lord knows I've done all I can possibly be expected to do. I can't do any more!

Jenny put her hands over her daughter's face and head protectively, pulling her warm body close to her own and burrowing her face into the tangled mat of curls, stifling a strong urge to run away, far, far away.

******

Suddenly she realized that daylight had come flooding into the space through an opened door, and all around her people were struggling back to their feet, brushing off their clothes and awkwardly wending their way outside, going back to their homes and their everyday lives. She noticed guiltily that none of them seemed nearly as traumatized as she had felt.

I'm glad I was too afraid to cry.

****

The days passed, one after the other, marked only by daylight and dark; and Jenny lost all track of time as they traveled steadily southward across the German countryside mostly by rail but sometimes trudging long distances by foot, simply following the crowds and the occasional Red Cross volunteer to the next station.

She was deeply grateful for all the unknown and unnamed local women, who seemed to appear from nowhere at many of the train stations. *These frauenschaft are truly angels,* Jenny thought, as she reached eagerly for the loaves of heavy dark German bread and thin cabbage soup they handed through the open coach windows. The women disappeared again as the train resumed its loud rumbling and clanking, moving ever farther southward.

"*Tuu, tuu, eiä, eiä,*" Marta sang the old lullaby very softly to Küllike. Then, as the little girl slept between them, the two older women discussed their future, speaking in hushed tones.

"What about our Estonia? Our home? Our friends? Will be able to go home when all the fighting is over?"

"Perhaps, Mamma, one day. But not until the Russians have returned our country to us."

"But, but, what if they don't?" Finally she voiced the concern that was always on her mind, "What about Vaike? How can we find her if we cannot go back?"

Both women sat in silence.

Vaike. And Oss.

****

"Oh, my, Jennie." Marta stood stock still in the middle of the paved street, holding Küllike's hand and looking around her.

Nestled in the beautiful, lush foothills of the German Alps, the stucco houses and, indeed, the entire area, seemed miraculously untouched by the shells and bombs that had scarred the towns and villages throughout the length of their travels.

"Can this be the right place?"

Jenny was feeling a little bit awed, herself. When they had finally arrived at Geislingen earlier that day, they were amazed to see that the area near the southern border of Germany had been untouched by the war; a stark contrast to the blasted landscapes they had been traveling through since they had left their homes oh, so long ago.

A briskly efficient woman, wearing a white cotton high waisted blouse with a badge reading: UNRRA / United Nations Relief and Rehabilitation Administration had explained everything. At least, Jennie felt sure the woman must have covered every single detail, because there had been an awful lot of information ... most of which she had forgotten or felt she had misunderstood almost immediately.

Jenny nodded to her mother, as she had nodded to the woman - rather numbly - and began to try to follow the directions she had been given.

****

One thing Jenny did understand was that they were required to stand in yet another long queue to register as Displaced Persons. Marta drew back instinctively when she saw that the long, improvised wooden table set up in the middle of the village was manned by uniformed soldiers. Jenny held her mother's elbow, steadying her and gently pressing her forward. "We're in the American Sector now, Mamma. These are American soldiers. They have promised to take care of us ... all of us, no matter where we're from."

"But, Jenny," Marta reasoned, "the Americans are allies with the Russians. And the Russians ... "

"Yes, I know, Mamma. But from what I have been hearing, the Americans can be trusted. But in any case, right now we have to do whatever the soldiers say. We just need to keep quiet and be careful." When Jenny saw that her mother still seemed unconvinced, she added, "And, besides, we can't get our ration cards or a place to sleep until we get ourselves registered."

****

Jenny saw the date written on the top of the first page of the many she would have to fill out that afternoon: October 4, 1944. She looked around anxiously, suddenly reaching out and sweeping both her mother and her little girl into a tight embrace. "Today is Küllike's birthday," she whispered into Marta's ear.

Both women were shocked; they had given no thought to the time of day, much less the day of the month, for weeks. Not since that frantic predawn in late September when they had begun their precipitous flight from their homeland; and that seemed immeasurably long ago.

Jenny quickly pulled herself together, released her grip, and turned back to the job at hand - taking care of the business of registering her small family so they would have a place to at least try to begin their new life.

13

Finally, Jenny and her mother and daughter were directed to the space that would be their home for the time being.

Although the two story stucco houses with a chimney at each end of the roofs and shutters at the windows seemed imposing from the outside, Jenny soon realized that each refugee family group would basically have one room. And they would be sharing the kitchen and the small toilet room under the stairs with other refugee families in the building.

"Oh, Mamma, this seems like heaven," Jenny sighed, as they finally lay down on the first real beds they had seen in such a long time. Even though the space was small, it was theirs.

"*Palju õnne sünnipäevaks,* little Külli," whispered Jenny to her drowsy daughter. "Happy Birthday, my dear child."

Snuggling together, Marta and her now three year old granddaughter were soon fast asleep; as were, judging by the chorus of snoring from the other rooms in the house, all the other displaced Estonians.

Except for Jenny, who, in spite of her almost overwhelming exhaustion, lay fitfully, thinking of her brave young husband. *Oh, Oss, I wish you could be with us today. I hope you are someplace safe; someplace where you are warm and getting enough to eat. I think you would be proud of me; of us. We have made it this far, and our beautiful little Külli will be safe here ... at least for the foreseeable future.* She sighed deeply. *Foreseeable future - I suppose there is no such thing.*

She finally drifted off to sleep, clutching her husband's wedding ring firmly in her hand, keeping it next to her heart.

****

The family that would be housed in the adjoining room, a man, his wife and their teen-aged son, who had arrived just before Jenny's group, brought them up to date the next morning.

"This sector of Germany is being administered by the Americans. They'll be responsible for seeing that we have food and shelter," the man who identified himself as Edgar explained. "General Eisenhower gave the German Nazis 24 hours to leave their homes in order to provide a place for us. They were ordered to leave everything behind, including their furniture and kitchen equipment, for our use."

"Come, Jenny and Marta, we will meet with the others who'll be living here, and we can get ourselves organized for sharing the kitchen and bath," his wife, Helina, added, smiling and nodding as she guided them down the stairs.

In a remarkably short time, the Estonian women who had fled their homes under the threat of imprisonment or even death, had set up schedules and guidelines for living together peacefully in this totally new environment.

****

"Come along, you three." Helina beckoned to Jenny. "We should go now; time for a good long session in the big sauna." Marta and Jenny looked forward to this social gathering every week. They could relax and gossip to their hearts' content, as well as get themselves and Küllike really clean; something they couldn't do with the metal tub they used to bathe with in their apartment during the week.

"Oh, Memme, I don't want to go," Küllike protested, futilely, every Saturday. "I don't like being in the middle of all those women. They're too big and too pink and too loud."

"Come along, Külli," Jenny would reply sternly. "This is my favorite time of the week, and besides, it's how I find out what's going on in the camp ... and the rest of the world. That is very important for us."

Küllike was unimpressed by the logic. "It's too hot, too," she added with a pout; but she went along, anyway, dragging her feet a little and looking around for any distraction that might delay their progress. No luck. She had to go in.

The higher row of benches in the sauna were the hottest, and Jenny often chose to sit there as long as she could stand it, while Marta chose the middle. Little Küllike stayed as near to the floor as she could, squatting beneath the fragrant hot steam and dashing outside just as soon as her grandmother had scrubbed her down and given her permission to leave.

It was during these sauna sessions that Jenny and Marta found out that the Americans who were assigned to look after the Estonians, as well as the Latvians and Lithuanians, who were quartered nearby, allowed twice as much food for the refugees as they allotted for the subdued Germans. It seemed the Americans were doing all they could to make it up to the refugees for the damage that had been done to them by the forces of war.

They also kept up, as much as they possibly could, with developments ... social, personal, and political, in their home towns and villages.

"Have you heard?" was a commonly used conversation starter. There was always news to be shared, and the women depended upon each other in their efforts to get themselves and their families organized, fed, and clothed.

"Have you heard that the distribution center has started getting powdered milk for us? It comes in boxes, is easy to ship and store, and we just have to add water."

"Have you heard? If you take your loaves to the bakery in town you can use their big ovens."

"Have you heard? The apples on the trees just outside the town are starting to get ripe."

And so it went; and of course Jenny and Marta would not dream of missing a Saturday sauna.

****

One of the apartments nearby became the distribution center for the rations, and Jenny was always able to exchange their coupons for enough basics to provide soup and bread for her family at least twice a day. There was rarely any meat, and the vegetables were scarce and scrawny because the countryside had long ago been stripped of all its crops and livestock to feed the German soldiers, but knowing that they would have something to eat every day was a well-appreciated blessing.

The center became a meeting place, a center for gossip, and a hub for the distribution of news as well as of goods.

One small bit of news Jenny was able to glean from home was terribly distressing. Her cousin Karl, who had been studying to be a doctor, had been sent to Siberia, simply because he had served in the German army during the Nazi years.

Siberia. Jenny shuddered. *Karl was like a brother to me; he even stood up for me in our wedding. He can't be in Siberia!*

Then, *Oss.* Jenny's mind turned from thoughts of her cousin to thoughts of her husband; she felt like she had been physically struck in the stomach. *Oss, my dear Oss, where are you now?*

****

There was a constant shifting and reshifting of accommodations, as more refugees poured in every day, but eventually the neighbors in Jenny's building reached a functional balance whereby they shared their talents as well as whatever goods they may have had to use, consume, or barter with.

Edgar and his lanky son, as well as the other husbands and teenagers, provided muscle for those jobs too heavy or cumbersome for the women; in turn the women knitted, crocheted and sewed, as well as cooked and cleaned.

When anyone was ill, as they often were, especially the first winter when everyone was still suffering from the harsh conditions they had had to endure, it was usually the women who nursed each other. They were lucky, though, to have a number of physicians among their number, so they had good advice, if not much in the way of pharmaceuticals or medical equipment.

Küllike, happy to be surrounded by an almost limitless supply of playmates, quickly adjusted to her new environment. Because the living quarters were so cramped, all the children played outside most of the time, watched over by any number of "aunts" and "uncles."

Marta was skillful and clever with the knitting needles she received in barter with another grandmother in the camp, and she picked apart outgrown sweaters and re-knitted new mittens and scarves for them all with the salvaged yarn.

The women found pleasure ... and comfort ... in keeping their colorful Estonian patterns in the articles they made.

14

The days went by in a jumble, but an increasingly more organized jumble, as the inhabitants of this hastily put-together camp and the American soldiers assigned to feed and shelter them adjusted to their situation.

The Allies, in each of the sectors of Germany, considered the Displaced Persons Camps to be temporary; there to provide assistance for the refugees until they could return to their respective homelands. Stalin was especially determined to expedite the return of "his" people.

On the face of it, this was a logical and noble plan; but it struck deep fear into the hearts of the Estonians, who had fled their country because of cruel oppression, and whose oppressors were still very much in control of the lives and property of the Estonians still living there.

****

Jenny was adding boiling water to the big cauldron in the cellar as Marta was scrubbing one of their bed sheets on a washboard. Swirling steam filled the space, finally wending its way through the open door and out into the cooler outside air.

Although working with the heavy, hot, wet articles was physically demanding, neither woman really minded the labor. They actually found the repetitive, predictable motions relaxing, because they could chatter to their hearts' content while they worked.

Suddenly a shadow blocked the sunlight, and they looked up to see their neighbor Helina hurrying down the steps. "Come quickly!" She was talking even before she arrived on the bottom step. "Hurry!"

Dropping the laundry back into the tub, Marta and Jenny scrambled up the steps behind their friend, each reaching out for one of Külli's hands as they hurried past her in the yard, bringing her along without missing a beat.

They asked no questions, and when they reached the silent crowd standing near the edge of the Latvian section of the camp, they remained quiet, but with every sense on high alert.

They saw a sad, scared group of their Baltic neighbors climbing stiffly onto a military transport truck. Although none of the group uttered any protest, the glitter of tears in their eyes was obvious in the bright winter sunlight.

One American soldier, who seemed to be supervising the loading of the human cargo, stepped up, raised and latched the tailgate with a decisive clang, signaled to the driver, and stepped back as it drove off raising a small, forlorn cloud of dust.

The crowd, many of whom were openly but silently crying, stood frozen until the truck turned the corner out of sight. Then, slowly breaking into smaller groups, the Latvian refugees started walking back to their quarters, talking in hushed tones.

Jenny and Marta and Helina also turned toward home. They did not speak until they were inside their own building again, and even then they were whispering.

"What just happened, Helina? Where were the soldiers taking those people?"

Looking over her shoulder to be sure no one was listening, the woman answered carefully. "They are being repatriated."

"Sent back to Latvia, you mean?"

"Yes," she affirmed. "Back to their hometowns."

"But," Jenny started to protest. "They *can't* go back; not yet. The Russians are still there. They won't be safe; they'll be ... "

"Yes. You are right," Helina agreed sadly.

"But why? Why would the Allies send them straight into danger? Don't they understand?"

"No, they really don't. The Americans think we all just left because of the danger of the fighting and bombing. They think we should be happy to return to our houses and farms, and they are doing their best to get us all resettled."

"But, that's not it! That's not it at all. We left because we heard that our family's name was on Stalin's *List* ... because I worked for the Germans, and because my father's family had ties with Germany long ago. They consider us sympathizers. Of *course* I worked for the Germans ... they had been in power in our country for the last four years!" Jenny stopped to take a shaky breath. "The minute those Soviet tanks came down our street, our lives were in immediate danger. It would be just the same for us if we had to go back now."

The laundry sat cooling in the tub, forgotten as the women sat on the cellar stairs, as close together as they could get, each lost in her own thoughts and fears.

"What if they tell us they are taking us back to Estonia? What can we do? We know our lives will be worth nothing if we re-cross our border."

It was Saturday again, women's day at the sauna.

"Should we just explain to the American soldiers? They seem kind; I'm sure they'd understand that the Communists have taken our Estonia against our will." The young mother who spoke was the newest arrival; she did not yet fully grasp the ramifications of her plan. She had not seen the truck disappear down the street in the Latvian section of the camp.

"No, we can't say anything ... the Russians and the Americans are allied; whatever we say to the Americans will surely be passed directly to Stalin's forces." An older woman spoke up urgently, her voice kept low by long habit.

"Yes, we must be very careful what we say," earnestly added another.

"I never know exactly how to answer all those questions the soldiers keep asking us."

"I know. They are so insistent about knowing every little detail about our lives, what we did, where we lived, what our political beliefs are, and what family we have still living there."

"And we all know that if we go back they will ... they will ..." the woman could not bring herself to finish the sentence.

The entire group sat in hushed silence. Even the small children sitting at their mothers' feet seemed to feel the gloom that had settled over the hot, steamy room, and ceased their happy chatter.

15

Once again, Jenny's family was on the move. As the continuing waves of homeless, stateless humanity poured into the area, accommodations at Geislingen had become more and more crowded and untenable.

Another Displaced Persons camp had been set up, and Marta and Jenny had been reassigned there. This time they had a few more belongings to take with them than they had taken when they fled from Põltsamaa, but not much.

Once more, Küllike's little doll Evie was tucked into her pocket – now with new clothes and a few more pieces of yarn for her hair - and once more Jenny carried Oss' heavy winter coat over her arm; and once more, each carried one bag with clothing and not much else in it.

They soon arrived at the Estonian section of Haunstetten camp, where things were running a bit more smoothly, but where the devastation of war was more evident in the surrounding area.

****

"Oh, my, is there never going to be an end to the questions?" moaned Marta, as they stood in another long queue waiting their turns to be evaluated and inspected and interrogated by the American military.

Both women tightly clutched the identification papers that they had been issued in Geislingen. These pages were all they had to show for all the lines they had already made their way through; they hoped that this different group of American soldiers would accept the information already set down, and not make them start over with all the explanations. But they knew that there would be even more questions, different ones perhaps, and that they had to be alert.

"Remember, Mamma, you can tell them that you're a widow, and I can tell them I'm married, but we must *not* mention that Oss was conscripted by the Red Army. They may use that as an excuse to send us back to the Russians. We must say simply that my husband is missing; and, and, that is true." Jenny paused, swallowing hard.

"When they ask us about going back, we can both say that we have heard that our town has been almost totally destroyed by the fighting, that our family has been dispersed, and that my job there no longer exists; therefore there is no place for us there now."

"Yes, yes, Jenny. I will be very careful what I say," Marta promised. "I well remember the truck we saw that day ... they say that none of those Latvian's friends here ever heard anything from them again after they were sent back." She sighed, shifting her weight from one foot to the other. Then, changing the subject to one more neutral, she added, "Oh, I wish this line would move faster."

****

Once again, they had to meet new neighbors with whom they would be living in very close proximity. They learned that the people assigned to the room next to theirs at the top of the stairs on the second floor included Linda, Peeter, and their young son Toomas.

Peeter had been a teacher in Tartu. He knew he would not be able to work in his chosen career in the German school system, but he told them he was hopeful that he and other teachers would be able to set up schools for the Estonians in the camp.

"That's a wonderful idea," said Jenny. "But what will you use for books? Surely none of us carried any with us when we left our homes."

"You're right. We don't have much in the way of educational supplies. So, I don't know yet," admitted Peeter. "But there are many teachers and other professionals in our number. We will surely find a way."

****

"Mamma, guess what?" Jenny came cheerfully into the communal kitchen, where her little girl was carefully helping Marta prepare a small cabbage for that evening's stew.

"Well? What, then?" Asked Marta, as she paused expectantly, holding her hands away from her apron to keep it clean.

"I've just heard that the Amann Thread factory in Augsburg is opening a few jobs for refugees!"

"That's wonderful, my daughter"

"So you think I should apply? There'll be a lot of competition for the jobs, I imagine."

"Of course, of course you should. Your experience working at the German police station in Põltsamaa should give you a good chance, don't you think?"

"Then it's settled; and I'll go to the city on the streetcar first thing tomorrow morning."

****

"Memme's home," Küllike squealed, and ran to hug her mother's knees.

"How did the interview go?"

"Perfect, Mamma. Better than perfect, in fact. Not only did I get a job, starting right away, but ... "

Marta waited, and waited ... "Yes? What could be better?"

"We have both been hired!"

"What? What do you mean?" Marta looked puzzled.

"You and I both can work at the factory, Mamma."

"But what about Küllike? Who will ... ?"

"Oh, that's the best part of all. They have a child care facility right on the premises. We can take her with us and she will be always nearby. We can even eat lunch with her every day."

Soon Jenny and Marta began to carve out a life for themselves; one that resembled, at least in the important ways, the life they had left behind.

****

From that point on, things were decidedly better for the small family. Of course, there were still shortages of food and goods, but now they had a regular income and could occasionally purchase fabrics and yarn and even, occasionally, a ribbon to make bows for Küllike's hair.

Küllike was playing tag with the other kids in the fields near the housing units, all of them wearing only their underwear because of the summer heat, when she spotted a man going to their building with several large boxes.

With excited squeals, the children quickly abandoned the game, and Küllike joined the others in swarming around the fellow. As soon as the door opened, she pushed around the man's knees and rushed to her grandmother. "Mamma, Mamma, what is it? Is it something for us?"

Marta shushed the girl and looked inquisitively at the man.

"It's a CARE package, Mrs. Rissman. The Red Cross volunteers in America have begun gathering small items and sending them here for us in the camps."

"Jenny, Linda, everyone. Come quickly," Marta called to the others, as she accepted the parcel for the building. "Sit, children, and be still," she shushed the throng of small folks.

When everyone was quiet, she set the heavy box on the floor beside her and untied the twine, carefully smoothing it out and setting it aside before she unwrapped the brown paper, then began removing the objects one at a time.

"Oh, look," she exclaimed. There are packages of powdered milk, and crackers, and even cookies."

The women of the combined household murmured to each other about each item, passing each from hand to hand around the group.

"We'll each have a little something extra to add to our plates this night," old Mrs. Vesilind sighed with pleasure.

"There are even American cigarettes." Marta held a package of Chesterfields aloft so all could see. "Even though we won't be smoking them, they will go far as a bartering item."

"And, that one pack must have ten or twenty individual cigarettes in it. If we open the pack and share the contents, that will be fair," added Astrid, from the downstairs room.

"I wonder what one does with this?" Marta held up a small, almost rectangular blue and yellow tin so the others could see it.

"Oh, that," laughed Aino, overhearing the comment. "I know it doesn't look like it, but that is cooked meat."

"No! Really? Meat in a can?"

Aino carefully inserted her fingertip beneath the small metal tab embedded on the lid, and pulled up with a flourish, peeling back the lid to reveal a pinkish sort of paste. Looking up at her neighbors, she grinned at their expressions of astonishment. "Cooked meat. Really," she confirmed.

"I've heard that you can mix it with anything." The young woman explained to the others. "Once you get used to the taste," she added, wryly. "Truly, it is a great source of protein, and you'll soon be looking forward to getting these precious little cans."

Marta took the can, vowing to cook with it that very night. "I'm sure it will make even our scrawny vegetables taste delicious!" she declared.

16

Küllike was in the middle of reaching for a large slice of the pretzel-shaped *kringel* that Marta had made for her when she heard Jenny's unexpected question.

"I'll bet you can't guess what is going to happen next week, Külli."

The girl looked up but continued wrapping her fingers around the special birthday morsel. Even though the sweet braided raisin bread had no raisins, and wasn't exactly sweet, either, because there wasn't enough sugar to sprinkle on it, Küllike well understood that the whole treat was in her honor; that this was a day just for her.

"What, Mamma?" she asked, shaping the word around the bite in her mouth.

"Now that you are four years old, you will begin going to school every day. Isn't that grand?"

Küllike stopped chewing a moment, and pondered this development. First she frowned just a bit, then broke into a sunny smile. "Like Toomas and Marje?" she asked

"Yes, you'll be in kindergarten with both of them, at the school Toomas' father organized."

Küllike was pleased, because this would mean she would see more of her best friends, instead of playing with them only in the evenings when she came home with Mamma and Memme on the streetcar from Augsberg.

"And you will learn to read and write ... and you can read to us soon, instead of your mother and I reading to you," Marta continued. "You are getting so grown up."

"And will I have a uniform like theirs, too?" Küllike had long envied the navy blue bib overalls that her friends wore to classes every day. Toomas' had solid blue pants and a checked bib; Marje's had checked pants and a solid blue bib with a checked border, like all the Kindergarten girls.

"Yes, indeed," Jenny assured her, reaching into the sewing bag at he feet and bringing out the uniform she had been working on for the last few evenings after her daughter had gone to sleep. "You will wear this every day."

"Oh, thank you Memme! I'm going to find Marje and tell her, right now," Küllike called over her shoulder as she ran out the door and down the stairs.

In less than a minute, she was back again, looking for the new wool hat that Marta had knitted for her out of yarn she had salvaged by taking apart an old sweater. Slapping it on her head, she pulled the sides down over her ears and ran outside again.

****

Marta brought the big enamel bowl over to the table, filled it with water she had heated on the stove, and began to wash their few dishes. Jenny dried each dish with a small towel and carefully stacked them on the shelf near the door.

"Can you really believe that she's getting so big already?"

"No, it doesn't seem possible," Jenny replied thoughtfully. "I remember so well when I first knew I was going to have a baby. I told the doctor I didn't believe him! But Oss was so happy when I told him; and I was happy too, of course." She paused, holding a forgotten plate in her hand. "Oh, Mamma, it seemed so wonderful then. We were so sure that if we just stayed out of everyone's way, that our life together would stretch out forever; that we would be able to keep our little family safe and full of joy.

"And then ... and then ... our little bubble was burst in such an abrupt and hateful way."

Marta saw the tears in her daughter's eyes, and felt her own heart breaking anew. While Jenny was mourning her husband, Marta's heart was breaking also for her younger daughter, from whom she had heard nothing since the day they'd had to leave their home in such haste.

"But who would have thought a year ago that we would be here now, safe and sound in Germany, under American care, and making an almost normal life with our little Küllike?" Marta gave herself a little shake, and made her voice sound reassuringly strong. "We're both working, she'll be going to school, and we have food and clothing and shelter."

"How lucky we are that we have this place, and that Peeter and the others were able to start the grammar school for our kids. Our little girl will have a fine education, a fine *Estonian* education," she emphasized.

"I know," Jenny agreed. "And now she'll have all those other activities, too, like drawing and singing, and organized games."

"Plus, all the students get those extra rations of powdered milk and sometimes even chocolates, I've heard," smiled her mother. "Things really are going well for us ... considering."

****

That very evening the two women joined a small group of parents who met after dinner a few times a week. Each adult carefully copied any books that they could find onto any scraps of paper they could gather. Sometimes they wrote the simpler kindergarten stories from memory. In this way they helped to provide texts for the students to share.

Everyone in the camp spoke Estonian, the teachers spoke Estonian, and of course the books were in their native language as well. Although they were in Germany, and surrounded by German-speaking people, the entire camp rapidly took on the feel of an Estonian village.

With less than ample food and clothing, of course. But since everyone was in the same predicament, those were considered to be minor discomforts

17

Küllike came home from school on a Tuesday afternoon with an extra sparkle in her eyes. She sat down and began speaking even as she was tugging off the winter suit that Mamma had made her from her father's heavy woolen coat. "They have started a Girl Guides troop, Mamma. May I join? I know it would mean extra work for you to make my uniform, but I can help. And I really, really want to."

"You have to promise you will keep up with your studies; you already have practices with the folk dancing group every week."

"I promise. Oh thank you, Mamma! Marje has already gotten her mother to agree, so this is perfect. This will be so much fun."

Küllike and Marje had become almost inseparable since they had become neighbors two years earlier. Even though the other girl was about six months older, they had been in the same classes all along. The two of them had so much in common, and loved to do all the same things. They both had short hair, and squirmed when their mothers put big bows on their heads for school.

When they could, they would run down to hike and play by the riverside, sometimes taking their baskets so they could gather berries to take home for their mothers.

And now they worked together on their scouting projects, doing crafts and learning to cook. Even helping their mothers sew their uniforms was fun because it was something all the other Girl Guides were doing, too. They had managed to make patterns out of old newspapers, and they used and re-used them until all the girls were properly attired as *Guides*.

With Küllike's' enthusiastic help, Marta sewed and knitted even more. They sometimes bartered for American Army blankets, which they dyed with their favorite bright colors and re-purposed into clothing that closely resembled the traditional skirts and vests that they had worn back in the old country, in happier times.

The commissary provided both everyday lace-up shoes and the black *mary janes* that the girls wore with white knee socks for special occasions.

Haunstetten looked and felt more and more like home every day, but the adults' hearts and minds were always full of both fear for the future and longing for the past.

Even though the older folks sorely missed having meat in their soups and stews, and badly wanted to have sugar just once in awhile, the children didn't really remember these things. They thought life was exactly the way it should be, and for them the neighbors, friends and homes they had left behind seemed less real than the ration coupons and barter systems that now shaped their daily lives.

18

Saturdays were women's days at the Sauna in Haunstetten, too, and Jenny and Marta always looked forward to the soothing steam.

"Did you hear?" asked Astrid Leps, switching a birch branch gently against her own bare back.

"You always ask that," complained the others. "Just tell us what you know; don't tease us every time."

"But it's so much more fun to be dramatic, don't you think?" Not waiting for the answer, which she knew well would be in the negative, Astrid continued, "All those questions we have to answer, and all those forms we have to deal with and all those endless details that

Flight to Freedom

the officials want to know ... it's going to be to our benefit, after all."

"How do you mean?" asked Jenny, who had complained as often as anyone else about these stressful inquiry sessions.

'Well." Astrid paused, looking around to be sure everyone else on the wooden benches was paying attention to her. "They're making up a master list."

"And? Why is that such a big benefit? They've been making lists since we got here, but we never see them."

"Don't you see? They will have everyone's name and other identifying information combined from all our directories into one big list. They call it the Registry. Everyone, in all the camps, even in the other sectors, will be named there."

When none of the other women seemed to see the significance of this right away, she spread her hands out in front of her, and explained with a small, exasperated sigh. "And yes, we can look at them ourselves. That means we can find each other. Those of us who have families that have been split up can look on the list and see if they are in Germany, and if so, which camp they are in!"

"I don't know," one of the older women mused. "There are thousands of us, and who knows how many camps."

Suddenly, Marta sat up very straight. "I understand now. This is great news! This means I can look for my Vaike. How soon will we be able to see this list? Where do I have to go to see it?" She could hardly sit still; she wanted to go out right that minute and start looking for her younger daughter's name.

Jenny put her hand gently on her mother's arm. "Yes, Mamma, this sounds like a good thing. But I'm sure there's not a copy of this 'list' ready for us to read just yet."

"But yes ... it, or at least part of it, is posted on the wall at the UNRRA's community building." Astrid looked as pleased as if she had invented fire. "Right now."

"Yes, yes, then, let's go, Jenny." Marta pulled Jenny to her feet, and as soon as they had dressed she practically dragged her older daughter down to the community building.

****

"I don't see Vaike's name anywhere," said Marta in a small, dispirited voice. "Let's just go on home."

"This can't be the final list," Jenny reasoned. "I'm sure the UNRRA ... and the Red Cross, too, see their logo at the top of the pages? ... will keep working on this. We will just have to keep checking every time they post an update."

"I suppose it would be too good to be true, to find that she is here somewhere, and safe. But I will never stop hoping."

****

The family did hear news, although it was of a different sort. Because of the thoroughly put together lists, Marta was able to receive word sent from her family still in Põltsamaa that her nephew Karl had returned from the gulag in Siberia, only to die of tuberculosis soon after he came home.

"He was so young, and he was going to do such good things as a doctor. Then to survive and actually return home from the Soviet camp ... then ..." She stopped.

"He stood up for me at my wedding! It seems so unjust," murmured Jenny.

"There has never been, nor will there ever be, anything fair about ..." Marta was going to say, *Stalin,* but thought better of it when she realized that someone was coming up the stairs. The by now well established habit of caution kept her from saying what she really thought. " ... war," she finished, firmly.

19

Every day Marta walked to the community building, even if she didn't need any coupons or other supplies, just to check the registry.

"So many names," she murmured as she turned away, disappointed once again. She knew the Americans had put a stop to accepting any more arrivals into the camps after April 21. It was October again already, and if Vaike had made it into Germany by that date, she would be safe.

But, on the other hand, if she had gotten into one of the camps, her name should have shown up on the registry by now. Hope grew increasingly dim.

One Friday evening, on her way home from yet another trip to check the registry, Marta saw her neighbor Astrid Leps, and they fell comfortably into step together as they walked along, comparing notes about what supplies each had been able to purchase or barter for that week. The two shared a kitchen and often traded recipes and ideas for new ways to prepare the scanty number of ingredients they had to work with to feed their families.

"It is almost our Küllike's birthday," Marta was saying. "I've been trying to save all the sugar that I've been able to get, so I can make her favorite *kringel,* but I know I won't have enough to get it made and taken to the village bakery shop for cooking by tomorrow."

Just then they heard a small commotion, as a group of children seemed to gather together out of nowhere, chattering and running down the street toward Marta and Astrid's apartment building. It took a moment or two, but the two women finally realized that the kids were following a man with a CARE package ... and he was going up their steps!

They hurried home to meet the fellow, and eagerly accepted the delivery.

Toomas separated from the group of youngsters and, waving goodbye to the others as they veered off to follow the deliveryman to the next building, bounded up the stairs right after his mother and neighbor, eager to see if this package would contain the usual boring things, such as tooth paste and toilet tissue and soap, or would it have at least one thing good to eat.

As Astrid cut off the string and pulled off the brown paper wrapping, the other two watched with intense concentration. She pulled out a blanket, a carton of powdered milk, instant coffee, and then, best of all from Toomas' point of view, a box of small chocolate bars!

"Wait, wait," his mother cautioned. "You know all the other children in our building will want some, too."

Toomas reluctantly pulled back his hand, which had been stretching eagerly toward the treats. "I know, Mamma," he said. "But I hope they come home soon!"

Astrid continued to pull out the precious items, carefully setting each can or package on the small counter beside the stove. "Oh, look, Marta!" She was beaming as she handed a small package to her friend. "Sugar." She smiled, waited a beat, and then handed her the very last box from the bottom of the carton. "And raisins!"

****

First thing the next morning, Marta was busily mixing, rolling out, and twisting the strips of dough, wrapping them in a small towel and setting them carefully near the hot stove to rise. When all was perfect, she sent Jenny to carry the special birthday treat to town to be baked in the big oven at the bakery.

When Jenny returned, with the delicious aroma of fresh warm sweet bread announcing her arrival even before she reached the others, she was in good spirits.

"Our timing was perfect, Mamma," she announced. "The owner of the bakery had almost decided not to open at all today, because the man who worked for him moved to a different camp to be closer to his relatives there. But then, in a stroke of luck (for him, and for us!) a new fellow showed up from Czechoslovakia, and he is an experienced baker, so they hired him on the spot.

"He had only just gotten there when I came in, and he spoke no Estonian, of course, but we were able to talk in German. When I explained that I had a birthday loaf for my daughter, he put on his apron and declared that he would take care of such a special *kringel* first thing. And he did. And here it is, perfectly baked," she added, pulling the towel from the beautifully browned twisted loaf with a flourish.

"Thank you, Mamma." Külli gave her grandmother a big hug. "And Memme, too. You always manage to come through for me."

She waved her hand across the air above the bread, wafting the aroma closer to her nose. "And I can tell it's going to be perfect," she declared with a broad smile.

20

Marta and Jenny and Külli were eating their supper in their room, thoroughly enjoying their meal of Estonian style *rosolje.*

"This is the best meal ever," sighed Marta. "It is so good."

"It is, isn't it? I was able to get good, red pickled beets from the market in Augsburg, that's why it's so delicious," confided Jenny. "Even without any meat at all, the taste still reminds me of home."

As they were eating, they discussed the "All Haunstetten D. P. Fellowship Night" program that would be coming up soon, and the costume that would be needed for Küllike. "I can get the fabric I'll need from Astrid, and we already have the thread. I'm sure I can have it ready by the time you need it," Marta stated confidently. Their heads were bent over the pattern that Marje's mother had drawn up for all the girls to copy by hand.

The door to their room opened slowly, and a head peeked in.

"Hello?" asked a very familiar voice.

Marta's hands flew to her heart, then up to cover her mouth, which had dropped open. She jumped up so quickly that she overturned her chair.

"Can it be? Is it? Really?"

The others, surprised at the older woman's reaction, stared first at her, and then turned toward the door more slowly.

"*Tere*, Mamma. Hello."

The door opened wider to reveal that it was, indeed, Marta's younger daughter Vaike standing there.

Marta rushed to Vaike and engulfed her in a strong hug; then with her hands on her daughter's shoulders, she pushed away so she could see the younger woman's face. Realizing that with her eyes full of tears she couldn't see her anyway, she hugged her again, even more tightly.

"Oh, my daughter. Oh, Vaike!" Marta finally managed to say. "I was so afraid ... I was so worried that you ..."

By this time all three women were in tears, and Jenny was pulled from her chair and into the group embrace.

After a few more minutes, and a lot more tears, Marta gently pulled Vaike into the room, righting the tipped chair with one hand and guiding Vaike toward it.

Only then did Marta and Jenny realize that Vaike had not come alone. Standing quietly in the hallway, waiting for all the women to quieten, stood Jaan Abraam ... and he was holding a little girl in his arms.

Seeing her mother's eyes widen, Vaike spoke quickly. "Mamma, you remember my friend Jaan, from home?"

Marta nodded, not saying a word.

"Well, he is my husband now. And this is our daughter, Karin."

Marta reached for the girl, who instinctively shrank back into her father's arms but kept her eyes wide open looking from Marta to Jenny and back again.

"Come in, come in. Welcome, Jaan. I am so happy to see you." Marta could hardly pull her attention away from the little girl, but she managed to find a chair for Jaan and offer the newcomers some coffee.

With all the excitement going on, Küllike had simply stayed put, remaining quietly seated on the edge of her little bed.

Eventually, everyone was seated, and questions, concerns, and reassurances were flying around the room.

"Vaike, I didn't want to leave before you came home," said Marta.

"That's true, Vaike. I had to make her go out the door. The tanks were coming down our street," Jenny emphasized.

Marta nodded. "They were so loud, my daughter. So loud!" Her voice caught in her throat, but then she continued, "We were so afraid."

Vaike patted her mother's arm. "I know, Mamma. I know. We were, too. We heard the tanks; they were too close to the house. We ran away, but the Red soldiers were everywhere! We had to hide."

"Then what did you do?"

Just thinking about their long, hard ordeal brought even more tears to Vaike's eyes. "We kept running, then hiding again. We could move around only in the dark, and we didn't dare walk on the roadway."

"What did you eat? Where did you sleep? And ..."

"Wait, wait," Vaike put up a hand. "We'll tell you all about it; and we want to hear your story, too, but right now I think we need to find somewhere for Karin to sleep. She is exhausted."

Küllike was still sitting on her bed, a little confused but also very interested in the stories she was hearing. She became aware that everyone was looking at her, and she involuntarily blushed. "What?" she finally managed to ask.

"Dear Külli, do you think you could share your bed with your cousin? You are both so small, I'm sure there will be room," Vaike asked, not unkindly.

No. No, I do not want to share my bed with this little person. I don't even know her. I never heard about any little cousin, and now here she is all of a sudden and they want me to let her sleep here? In my bed? No.

Although Küllike knew what she wanted to say, she also knew better than to say it. She managed to squeak out, "Okay," and squirmed over closer to the wall to make more room.

Jaan carefully lifted the already sleeping Karin from his lap and tucked her under the blanket; under *Küllike's* blanket. She opened her eyes and looked up at her *Isa*. He patted her shoulder, crooning the old favorite lullaby, "Tuu, tuu, eiä, eiä," until the girl closed her eyes again and began breathing in a regular, calm rhythm.

Eventually, even Külli had to go to sleep, and she allowed Mamma to tuck her in beside the other girl, as the voices continued to swirl around the room.

****

"So I not only have my lost daughter back, I have a granddaughter, too." Marta was so happy she was beaming, in spite of the fact that they had been awake all night, talking and crying and laughing and hugging and talking some more. "And a new son-in-law, too," she added hastily, smiling at Jaan. "I can't believe it. I just can't believe it."

"We thought we would never make it to safety," said Vaike, for about the third or fourth time. "We had to walk all the way from Põltsamaa to the coast; it took us forever."

"That's over 125 kilometers! Did anyone help you? With food? Or a ride?"

"No, no. We couldn't let anyone see us. There was no way to know who might help or who might turn us in to the Russians. You well know that even if we found someone who wanted to help us, they wouldn't dare."

"And we knew that would put someone else in danger, too," added Jaan. "And we had to stay away from the roads, except in the middle of the darkest nights, and then we had to be ready to dive into the woods if anyone came by," he continued. "Plus, it started to get really cold at night, and when we got wet in the rain we had no way to dry out," he said, with a shiver.

"We were so hungry. Always so hungry."

"Whatever did you eat?" asked Jenny.

"Not much! We tried to scavenge what had been left in the fields after the farmers ... and the soldiers ... had taken as much as they could." Jaan explained.

Vaike said. "But did you know, even if the apples had been on the ground for awhile, and even if they were full of worms and soft spots, and even if they were mealy-textured because they had been frozen ..."

" ... they were still the best things we've ever eaten!" interjected Jaan.

"Where did you sleep?"

"In the daytime, when it was too dangerous to be moving around, we slept wherever we could find a relatively dry spot, out of the wind. Sometimes we covered ourselves up with dried grasses and brush."

"We sometimes slept in farmers' barns ... that was the best, because the animals kept us warm."

"But scary, too, because if we both went to sleep and someone came in, there would be no way to get out without being seen."

"But sometimes we decided we just had to risk it, to get out of the cold and the rain."

"We were able to ... to uh, *borrow* a blanket from one of the barns, and that kept us warmer even when we were outside all night."

"We felt terrible about taking it, because we knew the family there needed it, too."

"But at least they had a house to sleep in, so we decided we needed it more than they did," explained Vaike, looking up at her mother.

Marta and Jenny took turns getting up to heat more water for tea, and the talking continued until the sun's morning rays came through the window and landed directly on Marta's face. Startled, she looked around at her family, nodded in satisfaction, and announced, "We are all going to sleep now. We will have more time," she stopped, and then finished, "lots more time to be together now."

Soon everyone was fast asleep, with Vaike sleeping with Jenny and Jaan settled on a blanket on the floor.

******

"Remember when we were so worried about all those questions and forms? Now I see that when they gave us our identification cards and told us not to leave the area, they weren't really putting us under any sort of confinement. They just wanted to be able to keep track of us." Marta and Jenny were walking Vaike, Jaan and Karin to the community building to see that she and her family were signed in properly.

"And that's how they were able to put together those registry lists," Jenny nodded.

"Oh, thank God for the American soldiers, the Red Cross, the UNRRA ... " Marta began.

" ... and all those volunteers who are doing all that paperwork that aggravates us so!" finished Jenny.

Marta stopped suddenly, in the middle of the street, and turned to embrace Vaike and Karin yet again. Then, a little bit embarrassed, she pulled away, straightened her jacket, and resumed walking. "I just can't help it; I'm so happy to have both my girls, and their girls too," she murmured to herself.

****

It took all day, but by suppertime Jenny had managed to not only get her sister and her family re-registered on the Haunstetten list, but also had made arrangements for all of them to be housed together in a slightly larger apartment in the same building.

Little Karin was enthralled by her older cousin, and wanted to be with her all the time, much to Küllike's dismay. "Mamma, I want to play with my own friends after school, not with ... " she saw the look on Marta's face, and sighed a small sigh. "All right. Come on, Karin, I'll help you put on your warm coat, and then we can go outside to play.

Soon enough, Küllike learned to love the smaller child; it was almost like having a little sister of her own. She rather enjoyed having someone to protect and care for.

Jenny knew that the two girls had truly bonded when she saw Küllike bring out her little well-worn doll, the one she had named *Evie,* and allow Karin to play with it.

Under her careful supervision, of course.

21

Life in Haunstetten Displaced Persons Camp became more and more like life used to be, back home in Põltsamaa, before the Russian annexation of their country.

Marta and her family had endured hardship and hunger, but had largely escaped the side effects of malnutrition and disease that still plagued a few of their neighbors. Now they had enough to eat, enough clothing – beautiful, Estonian-style clothing now! And everyone had a place to sleep.

Jenny still yearned for Oss, but the pain had become more of a steady ache instead of a piercing pain; she was able to truly participate in and enjoy the laughter and warm moments that she shared with her family and friends.

She had made friends with their neighbors, especially with Astrid, and the entire community was kept busy with music and plays and other performances, field trips and picnics, organized sports of every type, and walks beside the river for quiet times.

The overhanging cloud, now, was: "What next?"

The refugees had accepted that they would not be able to return to their homelands; the American, British and French authorities had finally understood that they could not honor Stalin's demands for the return of his citizens. It was a relief to know they wouldn't be sent back; but it still was a worry to wonder where they could go when the camps were disbanded, as they were sure to be.

Saturdays at the sauna; the conversations lately seemed to be focused on where the refugees would go next.

"I've heard that a few other countries have begun to say they would let us come in."

"I certainly hope so. We can finally believe that the Americans won't send us back to Stalin, but we know we can't stay in a DP camp forever."

"I've heard that Australia is opening up a little, but that they are looking only for able-bodied men."

"That won't help us ... we all have families!"

"I've heard that Canada might accept us ..."

"But they have restrictions, too, and all these places are saying they are going to have small quotas."

22

So, Jenny, do you want to go into town this afternoon?" Vaike asked matter-of-factly, pulling on her coat.

"Jenny?"

Vaike saw that her sister was standing very still, holding a paper in her hand, but not really looking at it.

"Jenny?" She asked again, going over to touch her shoulder gently.

When she still got no response, she took the paper and, seeing that it was a letter addressed to Mrs. Osvald Laumets, drew her breath in sharply.

Flight to Freedom

Dear Jenny,

I hope this letter finds you in good health.

I have had word from my brother-in-law who was also conscripted into the Russian Army in 1941, and he has asked me to tell you about your husband Osvald.

I am sorry to report that Osvald died in the fighting, less than 100 kilometers inside the Russian border, shortly after being taken from Tallinn.

So sorry to be the bearer of this sad news.

In sadness and love,

Your cousin, Hilda

"I knew it," whispered Jenny, barely moving her lips. "I knew when I never heard any more after that first postcard ... I knew he ... " She gulped, then dropped back into silence.

Vaike made soothing noises; not really words, almost a humming, and led Jenny to sit on the edge of her bed. She sat beside her, patting her back, then helped her lie back and pulled the blanket across her shoulders.

Tiptoeing out of the room, she met Marta in the hallway. "Oh, Mamma, Jenny has had news of Osvald."

Marta at first brightened, then she registered her daughter's tone and expression. "Oh, no. Is it bad?"

Vaike handed the written note to her mother in silence, waiting while she read it. They looked in to see that Jenny was apparently sleeping, then pulled the door quietly shut and left her alone to, hopefully, sleep for a while.

****

Jenny grieved in silence. She had been separated from Osvald longer than she had known him; their marriage and life together seemed more like a dream than a memory. But she was sad, so sad, to think of the way he had been taken, and the suffering he must have endured. She often stroked his ring, which she still wore around her neck on a small golden chain. She thought often of his overcoat and his words when he had left it with her. "Here, you keep it for me till I get back. I won't need it. The army will provide me with a uniform, which I'm sure will include all I need."

Sometimes it made Jenny more angry than sad. *How could Stalin do that to healthy young men? He took them illegally, just to waste them and throw them away, and for nothing! Just to keep them from fighting for the Germans.* At these times she would realize that her hands were knotted into fists, but she was powerless to act on her impulses.

Küllike never knew her father; Oss was just a name to her. But she soon learned that any mention of him would send her mother hastening out of the room. She was sad for her mother, but had no idea how to comfort her, so she mostly just left her alone when she had that forlorn look on her face.

Marta had never known Osvald, either, but she knew that he had been a fine man, and her heart was heavy for him – and for her elder daughter.

****

For the sake of her child, and her family, Jenny continued to participate in the activities and entertainments of the camp. Even though her heart might not be in it, she dutifully sewed and knitted and made clothing and costumes and uniforms for Küllike, and sat with Marta and the other parents to watch the performances put on for them by the children. She was proud of her family, and knew they had come through many hardships with their pride intact. *But I wish my family was intact; I wish Oss was here beside me.*

23

It was a warm summer evening, and a group of friends and neighbors were sitting on blankets on the grass listening to the Haunstetten Men's Choir perform, their wonderful voices rising to the clear, star-studded sky under the direction of a man who had been one of the best known conductors in all of Estonia.

As the first notes of the beautiful, *Mu isamaa, mu õnn ja rõõm* ("My fatherland, my happiness and joy") floated out to the crowd, first one person, then another, then all, rose to their feet and joined in.

Considered to be the official national anthem since Estonia's recognition as a free country in 1920, then banned by the Russians under penalty of deportation to

Siberia when they annexed Estonia in 1940, the song lifted everyone's spirits.

As the last note faded away, the crowd began to disperse, breaking into smaller groups and starting the pleasant walk home.

Marta sighed, as she was gathering up their blanket and food basket, "I love that song. It makes me proud, but it also makes me sad. It is beautiful to have the freedom to sing it out loud and in public here, but I wish we could go home, and sing it freely there."

"I agree," Marta's friend Anne said. "Hearing the anthem being sung openly and proudly is a very powerful experience. But going home again is just a dream."

As the group headed down the street, each lost in their own thoughts of home and family left behind, Jenny felt a light touch on her elbow.

Turning, she saw the fellow from the village bakery. "Wasn't that a terrific experience?" he asked her.

"Emil? It is Emil, isn't it?" Jenny felt the beginning of a small smile. In fact, the first smile that had touched her face for a long time. "Yes, it was. I know it was our anthem that made everyone so nostalgic, but you must miss your country, too. Where are you from? I don't think I ever had the chance to ask you."

"Tschechoslowakei," he answered, speaking in German. "And your name is ... ?

" ... Jenny," she replied, also in German. "This is my daughter Küllike, and ... " She laughed. "I was going to introduce you to my mother and sister, but it looks like they have gone on ahead."

"Hello, Küllike," Emil bowed and took the little girl's hand. "I am so pleased to meet you."

Küllike blushed just a little at the attention, but she was pleased. Even though the man spoke in a different language she understood him perfectly. This was the first time she had been treated as an adult in an introduction to a friend of her mother's, and it felt good.

As the three walked toward the apartment, Emil admitted that he knew Jenny's name already. "I couldn't help but notice you whenever you come into the shop," he confessed. "I heard that you had been widowed; I want to tell you how sorry I am that you have been made sad."

Jenny nodded, and felt herself engulfed again in the sorrow she felt for Oss. But after a moment, she gave herself a little shake, and allowed the feeling to fade a little.

"Were you a baker in Czechoslovakia, too? And where did you learn to speak German? And ... "

****

Jenny and Emil immediately felt that they had known each other forever. They had many shared experiences, but also so many new things to learn about each other. He made her laugh; and that was a very good thing.

The next time a family left from the building where Jenny and her family were staying, Jenny was able to arrange for Emil to take part of the space that had been vacated. It worked well for him; he really enjoyed being included in their extended family's activities, and they enjoyed having him there. Marta, especially, understood how important he was becoming to Jenny, and she welcomed him wholeheartedly.

And Küllike, well, Küllike bonded with him right away. He listened to her, and took her seriously, as well as having the easy ability to bring her to giggles.

****

Every time Marta or Jenny went to the commissary, or to the sauna, or to any of Küllike's scouting or school events, the conversation of any group in which they found themselves increasingly turned to the question that was on everyone's minds: *Where do we go from here?*

Finland, Sweden and France had slowly begun to open their doors for refugees, but only for a few.

"I've heard rumors that America might open their doors," said Anne.

"Australia, too," added another. "I think if I can choose I will choose one of those."

"But those are not available yet," cautioned Marta.

"But some are going to go to Canada."

"I think if you go to Canada you have to be a farmhand."

"I heard that Peeter Hendrikson was accepted to go to Belgium ... he had to agree to work there as a coal miner."

"I think I would agree to work on a farm ... or even as a coal miner if I only knew where I'd be going!" There were many voices, but the last was that of a middle aged woman; the import of her statement caused the others to hush for a moment, then they all started talking again at once.

****

Jenny was sitting with Emil with her head tilted earnestly toward his, as they discussed the future.

"Emil, it looks like all of us will have to go *somewhere;* they say they will close the camps within the next year or two; and I realize that my family will not be able to go to our, our ... home. I've heard that the house we lived in was totally destroyed by the Soviets, but so long as Stalin has control, there will be no place for us anywhere in Estonia.

"Do you have any idea where you might go?" Emil was concerned.

"Not yet. Everything is in limbo." She sighed. "How about you? Do you have a plan.?"

Emil shook his head. "No; every time I think an opportunity is opening up, either the slot is already filled or the restrictions are too stringent."

He started to say something else, but hesitated too long, and the moment passed.

"Well, we had better get these bags of supplies home; Mamma will be wanting to start supper soon." Jenny stood and began to gather their bags.

Emil said, "Here, let me take those," and they walked up the path to the apartment where, in fact, Marta was waiting for the package of cornmeal and the powdered milk, so she could make flatcakes for them for their evening meal.

24

At last!" Jenny came cheerfully into the kitchen where Marta was bending over the cook stove.

Looking up, Marta saw Jenny's big smile. "Yes?"

"I just heard down at the commissary that President Truman signed a paper that will allow 400,000 refugees to enter the United States!"

"That does seem to be good news," agreed Marta. "That is finally a realistic number, not just those dribs and drabs that the other countries have been offering. But, is there a catch?"

Jenny's smile faded a little. "Well, yes, of course. Isn't there always a catch? I don't know the details yet.

But anyway, with Australia already opening its doors, along with the other countries with their token numbers, we may actually be able to resettle before too long!

"Oh, I am so tired of being at loose ends, not knowing what or where our next home will be. I just want to know."

Marta nodded; she did not need to say a word.

Jenny knew that her mother, as well as the entire population of all the DP camps, felt the same way.

****

"This time my news from town is not so cheery," began Jenny one evening. "We are going to move ... again ... but not to a new permanent home. We will be going to Hoffelt Camp ... this week."

The family groaned at this announcement.

"With so many people relocating to new permanent homes, the officials are consolidating those of us who are left into the smaller camps," she continued.

"I don't mind moving; I just wish we could stay here until we make the big move that we know will be coming at some point," commented Vaike, wearily.

The others agreed, but all knew that they would gladly relocate a dozen times, maybe even a hundred times, if it meant they would not be sent back to live under Stalin.

Even though this move was just to a neighboring compound, each member of the family still had to stand in lines, again, and give their information, again, and be physically screened, again.

"I must admit," Marta said, as they were waiting in another queue, "I feel much less impatient with all this information gathering since I realize that it was precisely through all this effort that you and Jaan were able to find us. Once you two made it to Germany and were sent to the British sector, you would have never been able to track us down here if it hadn't been for the Registry."

"Exactly, Mamma," agreed Vaike. "And the same people who made sure we were all registered and accounted for were the ones who arranged for the military truck that brought us to your door."

"For which I will be eternally grateful," added Marta.

****

"Jenny," began Emil. "I am afraid that the authorities will send me back to Czechoslovakia."

Jenny gave a little start, but said nothing, just waiting to hear what he had to say.

"And if they do ..." He swallowed audibly. "I may never see you, or Külli, or your family, ever again."

Jenny looked down at her hands, clasped together tightly in her lap. She felt an almost overwhelming sadness settling around her heart.

"And I don't think I can let that happen. I know I cannot let that happen," he emphasized.

"But what can we do?"

"Jenny. My dear Jenny." Emil moved closer and took both her hands in his. "Will you marry me?"

Jenny had so many emotions surging through her mind and her body that she could say nothing. She felt first love, then joy, then fear, then relief, and then love again.

"Jenny?" Emil's face as well as his voice showed his dismay at her lack of response. "Jenny? I'm sorry, I shouldn't have ... "

"No, no, Emil."

Now his face truly seemed to melt with sadness.

"Oh, Emil. I didn't mean, 'No.' I meant, 'Don't be sorry.' Of *course* I'll marry you!"

****

"Before we go talk to the justice of the peace, Jenny, we need to decide what we are going to say."

"What do you mean?"

"I'm afraid that if I tell him I am Czech, he won't allow the ceremony; he might even arrange to have me sent home."

"Then, let's tell him you are also from Estonia," Jenny said quickly. "We have finally convinced the authorities that my family can not be sent back; they know they will have to send us somewhere else." Then she added, "We will already be married before he can check everything out."

"That sounds so tempting." Emil lowered his head in thought. "But you know, Jenny, in reality, we may get in a lot more trouble if we don't tell the truth."

This wedding included no pomp and no ceremony, but it certainly included lots of joy. And it included the truth.

25

Y ou know, I'm happy for my friends who have places to go," Jenny sighed, " but I will really miss Anne."

"Oh, did her husband get a guarantee?" asked Marta. "Where'll they be going? I know that she had her heart set on America."

"No, not America, but Finland. That was their second choice."

"Well, they are lucky nonetheless. At least they know where they'll be going."

Jenny nodded. "It's hard to be in such limbo. I am going to be sad about leaving, but I *am* excited about going ... does that make sense?"

"Of course it does," boomed Emil, who had just come into the room. We all feel that way, I'm sure." He smiled widely. "But at least you and I and Külli will be together, wherever we end up."

Küllike was upset that Marje and Toomas had both left with their families while she remained behind. Her sadness was mitigated by the reassuring presence of her new *Isa,* however. *I would rather spend more of my time with my own family, anyway,* she reasoned to herself.

****

Marta and Jenny and Emil and Vaike and Jaan spent many hours tracking down information, and then comparing notes at the end of every day.

"I understand why we can't control where we want to go, but we need to all agree to put the same destination as the first choice on each of our applications." Jaan was the one who kept the others coordinated and focused. "And we need to be sure to keep all of our information consistent. That way we will be kept together ... I hope."

By now they all knew that the American system required a "guarantee" for each adult in each family unit. Not a guarantee from the country that they would be allowed in, but a guarantee from someone or some entity in America that there would be a job and a place to live waiting for them as soon as they arrived on United States' soil.

"I've heard that the Lutheran Churches have been working hard to arrange for guarantees for all the Estonians," Vaike announced after a visit with her friends down the street. "And the churches in America are very active on our behalf. I think that's wonderful; the more organizations that are working for us the better our chances."

****

After the girls were asleep each night, the adults would stay up late, speculating about their new lives.

Australia, Canada, the US; in fact any other country than the one they were born in or the one they had lived in for the last four or five years, was an unknown. They all heard stories about the differences in lifestyles and they all shared their worries about being able to make a living in a foreign country.

During the day, the girls did exactly the same thing as the adults had been doing; they compared notes and dreams and fears and speculated about their futures.

****

"Listen to this," Emil announced to his family when he had carefully opened a big, official looking envelope.

"St. Mark Lutheran Church, in America, is offering sponsorship to our family."

"America! This will be a dream come true!" exclaimed Jenny, and Marta agreed, nodding vigorously.

"They guarantee that we will have a home to live in, and that I will have a job. This means I will be able to support us," Emil continued soberly. Then, looking up with a huge smile, he added, "This will not be charity. And that is important."

****

"My letter says the same," announced Jaan, coming up the stairs with his letter in his hand, followed closely by Vaike and Karin.

"Really? Your letter is from ... from this same ... St. Mark Church? In America?"

When he nodded, Jenny reached out for her mother and sister. "We will all be together ... and in America! This is all that we had hoped for," she exclaimed. She and Vaike hugged each other, then hugged their daughters, husbands, and their mother, jumping up and down as an ungainly group.

"Where in America is this wonderful church?" asked Jenny, when they had all dropped down onto stools, chairs, and the sides of the beds.

"Polo, Illinois," Emil answered, carefully enunciating the strange-sounding words.

Since most of what they all knew of the United States centered on either New York City - which they knew was one of the largest cities in the world, or the far west - where they had heard that cowboys and Indians were surely to be seen everywhere - they had to find a map so they could look up where Polo, Illinois, was located, exactly.

"I know that Anne has a world atlas," said Jenny. "Run over to their place, Külli, and ask if we can borrow it. Quickly, now!"

They found the small town neither in New York nor the far west, but rather more centrally situated in what would be their new country.

"It seems to be approximately ... " Jenny scrutinized the small inset in the corner of the map, "two hundred kilometers west of the big city of Chicago."

****

"Now we have to go in for more screenings," sighed Jenny. "This time we will have to all go through the physicals, too."

Küllike groaned at this news. "Again? Do I need to go this time? Maybe kids don't need to go ... "

Marta patted her arm. "Yes, of course you do. We all do, even Karin. It'll be no problem for you."

"It'll be bor-ring," Küllike stated firmly. "It's always bor-ring. And I hate the DDT powder!" She, too, though, was torn between excitement and dread about the big unknown that was coming.

****

"Mamma, Mamma! We got our notice! It says we are to be at the train station on Wednesday." Vaike had literally bounded into the apartment. "We have to be packed and totally ready to go by then."

"All of us? The whole family?" asked Marta.

Vaike scanned the piece of paper she had been waving about, then said with a frown, "No, this just lists Jann, Karin, you and me.

"But I must go right now and tell Jaan," she continued, hurrying out the door.

A few moments later, Emil and Jenny walked in the door, and Marta was up out of her chair and rushing over to them with the anxious query: "Did you hear anything? Did you get your notice?"

"No, Mamma, not yet."

"But Vaike and Jaan and I did," protested Marta, as though Emil could make things change just by a word. "Maybe your names are on a list at the commissary?"

"No, Mamma, I just came from there, and believe me, I checked very carefully. No word yet."

"But ... "

"Mamma, no word yet," repeated Jenny, gently.

Emil turned to Marta, "Did I hear you say Vaike has hers?"

Vaike rushed in from the next room, beaming. "Yes, yes we did. We are leaving on Wednesday." She stopped speaking when she saw Jenny's face. "Oh."

"I'm sure we'll get ours tomorrow," Jenny said. "After all, we have left on shorter notice than this before."

****

The entire combined family was at the train station early on Wednesday morning, and they joined the large crowd of fellow expats who would soon be taking the first big step of their new adventure.

When their names were called, Vaike, Jaan, Marta and Karin gathered around a woman with an NNRA banner on a short pole. After their identifications were verified, each stood still while the woman tied a numbered yellow paper tag around the top button on their coats.

"Keep this tag visible at all times." The woman admonished. "All the way. It is necessary for the volunteers to know where to guide you at each way point."

Off to one side stood Jenny, Emil and Küllike. They had not gotten their notice. They had, instead, gotten the report from their physical exams, showing that Küllike had a slight fever, and they would not be allowed to immigrate until it had cleared completely.

The much diminished family stood very still until they saw the others waving to them from a window almost at the back of the train car. Waving back, Jenny, Emil and Küllike walked, then trotted beside the train until it blew its lonely whistle and chugged off into the morning fog.

****

"Why did they get to go, and not us?" Küllike demanded as she was returning to the apartment with her parents. "It isn't fair. We got here before they did. We've been here longer." She could not help pouting a bit, even though she knew she was too old to act like that. "Besides, I'm older than Karin. Now she will get to see America before I do!"

"I know, I know," soothed Jenny. "But you remember that little fever that showed up at your physical? Your *Isa*'s guarantee from the employers in America is very clear that anyone in ill health will not be allowed to come."

"But *Isa's* not sick," Küllike continued her protest.

"Well, since we are family, and will all be traveling together, the rule applies to all of us."

Subdued by the thought that the delay was somehow her fault, Küllike nodded and remained quiet the rest of the way home.

****

Finally the day came when Küllike's fever had gone, and the family received the coveted letter of clearance to leave.

This time, even though the family had few belongings to take with them, they had much more than when they had first come to Germany almost six years earlier.

"Think carefully about what you want to take," admonished Jenny. "This wooden chest is lovely and sturdy, but it will hold only so much."

"I think we mostly need our clothing," suggested Emil.

"Yes, and maybe one or two of these army blankets. They have been so useful to us for so many things."

"I'm sure we won't need blankets," Emil protested. "We surely will be provided with everything we need by our sponsor in America."

"Yes, but what if something goes wrong along the way?"

Jenny well remembered being so dreadfully cold during the nighttimes on their long flight from Estonia.

She had slept on the ground, on station benches, on floors, and on the cars of the interminable trains. She insisted that at least two blankets should go with them on this scary journey.

Emil finally capitulated, understanding at last his wife's deep seated instinct for survival, no matter what, and two blankets went into the chest.

****

A big truck carried the small family, along with a dozen more, to the train station. After several connections and way stops, they reached the port city of Bremerhaven.

"Will you go check the postings again, or shall I?" Jenny asked tiredly.

After almost a week in a transient camp, enduring ever more screenings and long queues, and once again being sprayed with the DDT powder that Küllike so detested to ensure that no one would bring lice, fleas, bedbugs or any other pests with them onto the ship, Jenny was beyond excited and now was rapidly approaching exhaustion.

"Emil, do you think we will ever really get to America? This process is taking so much longer than I imagined. What if something goes wrong? What if they won't let us board the ship? What if ... "

"Now, now, Jenny, it's going to be okay," Emil soothed. "Perhaps you can stay here and have a nap; I'll go look at the lists, and I'll take Külli with me."

"Would you like that, Külli?" Emil was always careful to include Jenny's daughter in decisions affecting her.

"Of course, *Isa,* I'd love to go with you. There's always something interesting happening down by the docks."

******

"Memme, Memme, we have good news!"

The clear voice of her excited little girl woke Jenny from a deep, satisfying sleep, and she sat up, stretching.

"What is the news, my darling?"

"We saw our names on the boarding list for tomorrow!" Küllike was practically dancing around her mother, and glowing with excitement. "*Isa* took me to see the big ship ... it's huge, Memme!"

Jenny looked to her husband for confirmation of the details, and soon learned that they would, indeed, be on the American troopship *General R. L. Howze*, leaving the port the following day.

"Jenny, on the passenger list we saw the names of displaced persons like us from Czechoslovakia, The Ukraine, Yugoslavia, Hungary ... all over. At least a dozen of the 700 or so are from Estonia."

"It's going to happen at last, isn't it?" Jenny murmured, squeezing her husband's and her daughter's hands.

****

"We just thought the German ship in Pärnu was big," Jenny remarked as they stood gaping up at the long gangway leading to the towering deck of the troopship.

"I'm not scared," declared Küllike; but her mother noticed she clung a little more tightly to her parents' hands.

PART THREE

Across the Atlantic

April 1950

"Give me your tired, your poor, your huddled masses yearning to breathe free ..."

Emma Lazarus, "New Colossus"
Plaque on the base of the Statue of Liberty

26

As soon as the family arrived at the top of the gangway, they were directed to go different directions.

"You, number 551 ... go aft; that way." The sailor was brusque but not unkind as he gestured to Emil. "And you women, you go forward."

"But we're together," began Jenny.

"Not for the duration of this crossing," said the man firmly. "Now please move along, don't hold up the line."

Jenny looked around and realized that, in fact, all the families were being separated in this fashion. *No, I can't let Emil go now. He's stood by me all this way. We need him with us.*

"Please. Move along."

Emil let go of Jenny's hand, and with an apologetic look over his shoulder, followed the other men toward the back of the ship.

Jenny steadfastly led Küllike in the other direction, both refusing to look back.

"Külli, you take the top bunk," Jenny directed when they reached the crowded space below decks. "You're small and can climb up there more easily than I. I'll be on the bottom one.

"Where is *Isa*?" asked Küllike. "I want him to have the bunk next to me."

"It seems they're putting all the men in one section and all of us in another. He'll be fine, Külli. Don't worry," she added quickly when she saw her daughter's face threaten to crumple.

They each put their small carry bag on the selected fold-down canvas beds and then sat down heavily beside Jenny's things, exhausted by the eventful day.

Cutting through the babble of voices, in many different languages, they recognized a few words of their familiar Estonian. Suddenly re-energized, Jenny jumped up and made her way through the throng of women, calling out, "*Tere, tere!*"

Two other Estonian women heard the "Hello," and began working their way toward Jenny.

"Let's try to stay close together," Jenny suggested to the others. "That way we can share any information we get, and our lives will be easier. I think there are a couple of bunks still empty near ours."

Introducing themselves as Dorothea and Mari, sisters who had escaped from the university city of Tartu about the same time that Marta and Jenny and Küllike had fled from Põltsamaa, the women were pleased at the prospect of joining forces for the duration of the ocean crossing.

****

When they felt the massive vessel begin to rock in a different way, and the big engines' rumbling seemed louder, all the women in the section began to go toward the deck.

Even though they were uncomfortably crushed by the crowd, no one wanted to go below decks; all wanted to watch the shores of the Weser River glide by as they made their way to the sea.

Will we ever see Europe again? Jenny wondered, but did not want to say her concern aloud. She just hugged her daughter closer and tried to stay upbeat about the adventure upon which they were embarking.

After the shoreline had totally disappeared, the crowd began to straggle back to their bunks, beginning to be more interested in filling their empty stomachs than in watching the gleaming sea rolling past.

The first meal was heavenly. It was a bit strange, and a lot crowded, and they weren't used to eating standing up, but it was heavenly all the same.

"Memme, what is this?" Küllike was holding up a bright orange, juicy slice of fruit, with a puzzled look on her face.

"I don't know either, Külli, but taste it and see if you like it."

The little girl gingerly licked the glistening wonder and broke into a big smile. "It's good!" She bit into the flesh ... and some of the rind ... of the orange. "Ugh. The skin isn't good at all, though," she announced.

****

By the next morning, Jenny and Mari and Dorothea had compared notes and found that if they went up to the deck right after they cleaned up the breakfast dishes, they could get word to their husbands.

When Jenny spotted Emil, after what seemed like hours looking for him, she rushed Külli across the deck. "Emil, I was so unhappy that you went away from me. I'm so glad ... *we're* so glad ... to see you."

Emil nodded, not wanting to show that he had missed his wife as much as she had missed him.

Dorothea's husband Jaak joined the group, too, and from that moment they all fell into a regular routine of eating, sleeping, helping with the kitchen and clean-up duties, and visiting with each other. Mari was a widow, and had lost her son in the war, but Jaak and Dorothea's daughter had gone on to America with her husband and children the previous month.

****

On the fourth day, the beautiful Atlantic became a raging, heaving beast. Seasickness was rampant among the normally land-bound passengers, and the results of their distress made it miserable for the others as well.

"Memme, let's move to another place. It smells really bad here," Küllike implored.

Emil and the rest agreed. They realized they were lucky not to be sick from the movement of the ship, but they were often almost ill from the odors that surrounded them.

Finally, the weather changed, the ocean calmed down again, and even those who had been suffering the ravages of seasickness were able to relax and join in the conversations about what they might find in America.

Marta, Vaike, and her family had probably landed in New York City about the same time as Jenny and the rest had been leaving camp, so they had received no word at all from her yet.

But Dorothea and Jaak had word from their daughter. "We received one letter; our daughter sent it from New York City as soon as she could. She just had a few quick impressions," Dorothea said. "She mainly said there were cars everywhere."

Jaak added, "And she said that when Americans smile, they show all their teeth. Doesn't that seem odd? She did say the people were helpful and friendly, though."

"I've heard that they have no saunas in America," added one of the other Estonian women. The group sat silently for a moment after that bit of news.

"No saunas?"

"Yay!" spoke up Küllike, but then she became quiet again when her mother gave her a stern look.

"How will we get along not being able to speak English?" Mari brought this up more than once.

No one really had the answers; they just had more questions, spoken and unspoken.

On April 3, 1950, their tenth day at sea, the mood of the entire civilian population of the ship became energized; they knew they would soon be coming, at long last, to the exciting, huge city of New York, which would be their gateway to the exciting, huge country that would be their home.

"Follow me," Emil said, as he guided his family through the throngs of refugees on the ship's deck. "This will be perfect," he eventually announced when they finally reached the railing. "We should be able to see the city's tall buildings soon as they come on the horizon."

"How long do we have to wait, *Isa*? Asked Küllike. "Can you see it yet?"

"No, no, not yet. We will just have to be patient a little while longer, my daughter."

It was not only Küllike who was fidgety; the whole family could barely keep still.

"Is that it?"

"No, I don't think so."

"How about there?"

"No, we will know it when we see it."

"Oh, no, it's starting to get foggy over the water. Maybe we won't be able to see anything until we actually dock."

Just as they were starting to feel really disappointed, Emil gasped. "There it is. There's the Statue of Liberty." He was almost whispering.

Jenny leaned into her husband's shoulder, with her daughter in her arms, and watched silently as the torch of the great lady emerged from the rising fog.

She could feel Külli rummaging around in her coat pocket, with an intent expression.

"Külli, quit whatever it is that you are doing. You need to look up and see this," she admonished.

Then she saw what her daughter had pulled out. It was the little, ragtag doll that had come with her from Põltsamaa, to Geislingen, to Haunstetten, and now to America. Küllike held Evie up high, both of them bravely facing the future.

Jenny smiled.

We've made it. We have found our freedom.

POSTSCRIPT

When Ku Adams finished telling me her story, she told me she had one more detail to add.

So, these are her words.

****

The only thing tangible I thought I possessed to remember the father I never met, Osvald Laumets, was the letter my mother had received from her cousin Hilda telling her of his death in Russia shortly after his conscription into the Red Army. I have kept it, very carefully, in a special scrapbook.

My Isa died in Washington, Illinois in 2012 ... and, yes, I considered Emil Sikula to be my father; I loved him dearly, and he always treated me as if I were his own ... anyway, I was staying with my mother after his funeral.

That night, just before we went to sleep, she asked me, "Ku, do you want your father's wedding ring?"

I said, startled a bit, "No, Memme, don't you think Harry or Tina or Eric should have it?"

She repeated, more firmly, "Küllike, do you want your father's wedding ring?"

I couldn't understand why she was so insistent. Of course, I would have loved to have had it, but it didn't seem proper for his ring to go to me.

After all, I thought, the three other children Memme had with Emil after we all arrived in America might be considered to be his real children.

Once more I declined, then she said, "Ku, this is your father's ring." She reached over for my hand, and put the simple gold circle on my palm.

"This is the ring I gave to Oss when we married in 1940; and I used the same ring when I married Emil in 1948. We had no way to get such a thing in the DP camp then, so I gave him this one, and he wore it for all these years.

"So, you see, my Küllike, it is right that you should keep it."

And I've worn it on my right thumb ... where it fits perfectly ... ever since, as a way to honor both of my fathers.

Books by
Marilyn Smith Neilans

"Saying GoodBye to
The Iris Lady"

And

"Flight to Freedom
One Family's Escape from Estonia"

Available on

Amazon.com

And

Neilans.com